The Mermaid

Short stories for adults

Penny Luker

First Published in 2012 by Bindon Books, Leyton, Cheshire, CW6 9JA

Printed by Lulu.

Acknowledgements

Many thanks to everyone who has encouraged and helped me to write this book. Thanks to Olwyn Dean and the members of our Creative Writing class at Mid-Cheshire College, for ideas and suggestions; to The Open University tutor and students on A 363; to Elizabeth Horrocks for helping to proof read the book and to my husband, David and my family for their support.

ISBN 978-1-326-92577-2

Contents

The Mermaid

Ralph strode along the cliff path on the outskirts of Ilfracombe. He could smell the freshness of the sea and a cooling breeze brushed against his face. He paused in his usual place and looked downwards towards an outcrop of rocks and there she sat; the beautiful mermaid with her shimmering tail, on the flattest rock, with her blonde hair billowing out behind her. He could tell she was beautiful even at this distance. She seemed to sit there every morning at this time. Of course he was just being foolish. She wasn't really a mermaid. She was wearing a purple patterned sarong that flapped in the breeze and gave the impression of a mermaid's tail. He thought she was young because of her slim body, which he knew to be agile as he had seen her dive into the sea.

This holiday was his way of drawing a line under the past year. He thought about how his life had changed. The bitterness he felt had not dimmed. He must do something to move on and find some peace. He twisted the gold band on his finger until it was free and then held it up to the sun. How happy he had been when Kate had agreed to marry him. He threw the ring as far as he could into the sea and it disappeared forever.

The mermaid was removing her tail and then she dived cleanly into the clear blue sea. She swam like a fish quickly and efficiently with smooth rhythmic movements. Soon she disappeared under the waves. The first day he had seen her do this he'd thought she had drowned, but he waited and waited and finally her golden head had popped up some distance from the shore.

He watched the sea and continued his walk along the South West Coast Path. As he saw her surface he turned back towards the hotel. Ralph spent the afternoon reading and researching. He could tell that the long walks, good food and working in this relaxing way were doing him good. The scenery was exquisite and the fresh air made him hungry.

He went downstairs at seven p.m. to the dining room and was greeted by the hotel proprietor, Mrs Mere. She was a tall slender woman with her fair hair wound in a knot at the back of her head.

'Good evening Mr Blake. I hope you've had an enjoyable day.'

'Yes, thank you, Mrs Mere.'

'If you would like some company at dinner, do say. I sometimes join lone diners.'

Ralph's head screamed silently, 'No!' He didn't want to make conversation with a stranger but he smiled at the proprietor and said, 'That would be lovely.'

She showed him to his table and said she would be with him in a minute. A warm vegetable soup was served as a starter and Ralph tucked into it enthusiastically.

'How are you enjoying Ilfacombe, Mr Blake?'

'It's very beautiful. I walk along the cliff path in the mornings and enjoy the views of the sea.'

'Ah, yes, I believe I've seen you. I often read my book sitting on the rocks before my swim.'

He looked at her again. She had the long blonde hair and the tall slim body. Before he could stop himself he said, 'Oh you're my mermaid.'

She laughed. 'I am a good swimmer. I've lived in this area all my life and the sea is very much a part of me.'

'I'm sorry. I do let my imagination run away with me sometimes. I'm collecting local stories and I was hoping to find a mermaid one for my new book.'

The waitress quietly appeared and filled their glasses, his with wine and hers with water.

'I will tell you a mermaid story but first you must tell me why you are so unhappy. I can feel it in you every time we talk.'

Ralph hadn't thought he wanted to tell anyone but she had a gentle, almost hypnotizing voice and he found her a good listener.

'It's a common story. My wife ran off with another man, after thirty years of marriage. It was about a year ago. I came on this holiday because I know I have to deal with it, and move on, but I find it very difficult. You see she left me for our son's best friend. He was always in our house. I made him welcome.'

'Perhaps you could try feeling sorry for her.'

'You think I should feel sorry for that cheating...' he began in a controlled whisper, lowering his voice in case he exploded.

'What's the age difference? Twenty years?' she interrupted.

'Twenty-five actually.'

'Although I believe that age is just a number, in human life experience, twenty five is a lot of years. Tell me do you wish to do the same activities as your son, even though you love him very much?'

'Well no. We go out now and again, but mostly he does his thing and I do mine.'

'It will be the same for your wife and her young lover. They'll increasingly find that they don't share the same interests and has she lost the love of her son?'

'Not exactly, but he doesn't really want to spend a lot of time with her.'

Mrs Mere finished the last of her vegetarian pie. 'Whatever happens in the future her relationship with her son will never be the same. I would feel sorry for her. If you change all that bitterness into pity you will be able to move on and find some peace. She has a lot of heartache ahead.'

'Next you'll be telling me she'll want to come home and I should forgive her.'

'I'd never dream of telling you any such thing, but I hate to feel your unhappiness. Now I promised you a mermaid story. It will give you another perspective on life.' She smiled at him and her face became so beautiful he could hardly take his eyes off her.

'Would I be able to use the story in my book?'

'Of course, but please don't acknowledge me. It is after all a legend.'

The waiter served up a light lemon mousse and poured more drinks for them both.

'The merpeople are often portrayed as wicked people who lure gullible men to their death, but this is never their intention. They used to sit on rocks to warn sailors of the perils of the sea and their screams of warnings unfortunately drew the sailors closer. Mermaids have always been fascinated by living on land and every so often one would fall in love with a human and go with him, but if she chose to do this she could never again live beneath the waves. One such mermaid fell in love and went to live with her man, who was an innkeeper. They were very happy together and then they had a beautiful daughter.

Children of merpeople can make the choice to live beneath the waves, but they can only make the choice once. This child was drawn to the sea. She loved it with a passion and one day she swam out to a rock and the waves called to her and she dived in. Her father swam after her. He was a strong swimmer but only a human. He tried and tried to find her but eventually he became too weak to swim and he died. So the mermaid was left bound to the land, having lost both her daughter and her husband and her sadness was immense. She was so sad she could feel any sadness in anyone who came near her and she always tried to help them. In fact it was only by helping others that the mermaid felt any relief from her pain. After some years, when she was walking by the sea, she saw a mermaid and knew immediately that it was her daughter. She swam out to her and although she can never live under the waves she can spend a few minutes every day with her dear child.'

'What a beautiful legend,' Ralph said. 'It will be the jewel in my book. Thank you.'

***

The next day Ralph packed his bags ready to go home. He took the cliff path. He would look at his mermaid one more time, but she wasn't sitting on the rocks. He searched the sea and suddenly he saw two blonde heads pop up. They made no sound but both waved their hands at him and he waved back. She had trusted him with a secret and it somehow healed him. He would tell her story but he would set it in a different time and place to protect her.

Mixed Messages

Li Wan was sitting in class thinking about his new laptop, which was being delivered today. The teacher was a complete idiot. He couldn't even remember the symbol for sulphur. Usually Li Wan helped him out but today he really couldn't be bothered. The rest of the class waited expectantly for him to intervene, but he didn't.

'I'll just look it up,' said Mr Blanch, 'although I would've thought one of you would remember.'

Still Li Wan kept quiet. With his new computer he'd be able to study online and then he might learn something. He'd wasted almost a year in Blanch's class. The man was a buffoon.

'But it's you who should know, isn't it sir? You're supposed to be teaching us,' said Li.

There was an intake of breath; not because of the rudeness. That was common in the chemistry class. It was because the teacher's pet was always so polite. He was never rude.

'I expect better from you, young man. I have the chemistry knowledge. I just have a poor memory. Ah, here it is; the symbol for sulphur is S,'

'I can understand you forgetting some of the symbols but S for sulphur!' said Li.

'What is it with you today, Li? Get out of bed the wrong side?'

Later that day Li Wan kissed his gran on the cheek when he got home. The mynah bird, sitting on his large perch, chirped, 'Good afternoon, Li Li.'

Li smiled and went over to speak to the bird for a few minutes. Then he turned to his gran, 'Any parcels for me?'

She passed him the brown package from Curry's and he was surprised how small it was. Then he looked at the name and saw that it was for a Ms Lulu Latiff, who lived about half a dozen houses down the road from his gran's house. He was so cross he felt like chucking the parcel across the room. *Why hadn't his gran checked it was for him?* But he knew the answer; her sight was failing so he couldn't really be cross with her. Disappointed he went up to his room to listen to music.

***

Lulu Latiff had squashed herself into a boob tube and mini skirt. She would open up the parcel from Curry's that contained her new camera and take some pictures for her model portfolio. It was a special camera with a remote control, which meant she could take pictures of herself, without having to go to some lecherous old photographer. Picking up the parcel, she was about to rip off the brown paper when she noticed that the name on the parcel was not her own, although the street name was correct.

I wonder if this is for that good looking Chinese boy? she thought. *If I have his maybe he might have mine.* The thought that she could get her pictures done today urged her on. Her watch said 18.37, which she felt was still early enough to make a call. She slipped on a skinny cardigan, put the parcel into her tapestry bag and set off down the road.

***

'Excuse me is Li Wan here?' she asked the old lady that answered the door.

'Yes, you must be one of his friends. He's in his bedroom. Go on up.'

Lulu hesitated for a moment and then went upstairs. She could see Li through the open door. He was listening to some music, lying on his bed. 'He is gorgeous,' she thought.

At that moment Li looked up.

'What are you doing in this house?' he asked.

Lulu fished into her bag and brought out her brown parcel. 'This has been delivered to my house and I just wondered if my parcel had come to yours.'

He could not take his eyes off her. She noticed that his cheeks had gone a little pink and guessed that she was not unwelcome. She stepped into his room and smiled.

'We need to go downstairs.' He said rushing past her out of the room, so she sighed and followed him down the stairs.

In the living room Li's gran smiled. 'Aren't you going to introduce me to your girlfriend Li?'

'I'm Lulu Latiff,' said Lulu when Li couldn't get a word out.

'Lulu Lulu Li Li Li Li Lulu Li Li,' said the mynah bird.

'Oh what a lovely bird. Aren't you the clever one?' said Lulu.

'Are you stopping for tea?' asked Li's gran.

Lulu looked across at Li and could see that he was interested in her but painfully shy. She might not ever have his academic brains but she had her own skills. She understood people and she understood herself.

'I don't want to impose, but if you're sure that's alright, I'd love to stay,' she said giving Li a smile.

Li Wang had never had a girlfriend, but he was a bright lad. Lulu was beautiful and happy to sit and talk with his Gran. She might be wearing next to nothing but somehow he'd learn how to deal with that. He smiled right back.

'Come and meet Jabberwocky properly,' he said pointing to the mynah bird.

So the special camera and the brand new laptop stayed in their brown packaging for a little longer.

The Perfect Bride

Sophia knew something was wrong but what should she do about it? Rupert wouldn't look her in the eye. He was avoiding spending time alone with her. She examined the last couple of weeks. They hadn't rowed and she couldn't think of anything she'd done to annoy him. The problem was there was no time. The wedding was tomorrow.

The next day dawned with a clear blue sky. It was a perfect day. Sophia bathed and started dressing herself in all her finery. The dress was so beautiful. She decided that if Rupert had a serious problem he would tell her and having made that decision, she was going to enjoy the day. They had spent a year planning their wedding; the venues for the ceremony and the reception, the flowers, the food, the clothes and the honeymoon.

The church was exquisite, decorated with white roses and packed with people. Rupert stood at the end of the aisle looking as handsome as ever. Sophia paused and straightened the folds on the long silken gown. Then she linked her arm with her father's and the music started.

After the service Sophia and Rupert stood together ready to walk up the aisle but standing in their way was Marcia, the chief bridesmaid. The deep mauve satin of her dress showed up her very pale face.

'Well that was a perfect wedding, wasn't it? A perfect wedding for a perfect bride. Rupert has told you that he and I are lovers I presume.'

'Well...hardly that,' said Rupert.

Sophia looked at Rupert and knew immediately what he had been trying to hide.

She took a deep breath. 'Of course he told me all about it. He said he regretted it totally and so I had to forgive him. Will you let us pass please? We have a reception to go to.'

'It's not such a perfect day now though, is it?' said Marcia with a little glint of malice in her eyes.

'I'm not sure why you would want to hurt me, Marcia, I thought we were friends.'

'Friends? How can anyone be your friend? You spend so long planning to get everything perfect you don't have time to be a real friend. You don't love Rupert. You wouldn't just forgive someone who betrayed you. No, but you'll forgive him because you think you both look good together. He'll still fit in with the life you planned.'

Suddenly a loud voice boomed out; it was Sophia's father. 'That's enough Marcia. This is neither the time nor the place.'

Marcia looked at them all, was about to speak and then decided against it. She stepped aside.

Sophia re-linked her arm with Rupert and they started to walk forward.

As soon as they were in the car Rupert said, 'Thank you, so much for forgiving me. It was only once. I don't know how it happened. I'd just drunk too much.'

Sophia said, 'I could see you were really sorry. I knew there was something wrong. You couldn't look me in the eyes.'

'Oh I am sorry and I'll never let you down again.'

They arrived at the hotel where the reception was to be held. Rupert got out of the car and went round to open the door for Sophia.

'Sorry, I'm just popping home to get changed. Make my apologies. I'll be about half an hour Rupert and then I'll feel better in something less dressy. I won't be long.'

'OK my love. I'll be missing you.'

Sophia, let the driver of the car take her home. Quickly she changed out of her beautiful gown and picked up her bags, passport and the air tickets. Then she persuaded the driver to take her to the airport. She may not have had the perfect wedding and she certainly wasn't going to have a perfect marriage but she decided she was going to have a perfect holiday.

The Collection

She was there again today. He took a seat opposite her and she smiled. He liked women who were bold and he smiled back. A large woman squeezed into the seat next to him and the train rattled out of the station.

He looked at the woman again. She was reading a newspaper. He admired her long elegant neck and the white blonde hair, so like his mother's used to be. Perhaps he would ask her out tomorrow. He liked meeting women on trains, or anywhere away from the village, because they didn't know his family or the dark cloud that hung over his life, which blighted his meeting women. Who would want to go out with the son of a murderer, still on the run?

He could feel the warmth of the fat lady against his thigh. *Disgusting.* He moved in his seat and crossed one leg over the other to get away from her, but she expanded into the extra inches. The train became more crowded at every station. It was a relief to breathe the cold air as he stepped onto the platform. He hadn't asked for a date; maybe tomorrow.

Suddenly he felt a hand on his arm.

'I don't suppose you fancy a drink or a meal after work,' the young woman asked.

He noticed her slim legs and delicate ankles and the very high heeled shoes as he turned round to speak to her.

'I can't make it tonight. What about tomorrow? I'll be free by six-thirty. What about you?'

'That'd be lovely. Shall we meet at the station entrance?'

'Yes, see you at 6.30 tomorrow, although I'll probably see you in the morning on the train.'

***

The next day he was ready for his date. He had his smart brown leather hat and gloves in his briefcase and a well tailored raincoat to wear on the late train home. His mother always visited her friend Betty on Fridays so the night was his to enjoy. Before he left for the train he went to the basement and looked at his collection of shoes. People collected all sorts of things these days; you only had to look at the antique programmes on the television. His little collection barely took up one shelf of the cupboard. It was a private collection, which was why he kept it in the basement. It was the one place in the house that was his. The rest of the house was his mother's. She'd even go into his bedroom on the pretence of tidying it and she would ferret through his things. He knew because she never put things back in the right place. The joke about it all was that his mother didn't do housework. She didn't cook. She only used the kitchen when he wasn't there to wait on her hand and foot.

Of course he'd challenged her about her prying but no-one ever won an argument with his mother. The basement entrance was the back wall of the disused larder. His mother didn't even know it was there. The shelves on the back wall hid the fact that it was a door. He was a man, not a child and he needed his own space. The basement wasn't luxurious but he had a few home comforts. There was a comfortable old chair and African rug, his collection cupboard, which also contained music and DVDs, a fire and a good bottle of malt with a crystal cut glass. He'd smuggled most of it down there on Fridays when she went out to her friend Betty's house.

He went over to the cupboard and admired his collection of shoes. He liked the different textures and colours. The minutes passed and suddenly he realized he was late for the train. He rushed off to the station to see his train trundling off into the distance. It was going to be a long day.

At six-thirty he was standing waiting at the entrance to Charing Cross Station, wearing his hat, coat and gloves. It made him feel more distinguished and the women seemed to like it. It was still busy and he wondered if she would come. Then he picked her out of the crowd; there she was walking towards him. Her skirt showed off very long legs. She smiled at him and his heart lifted for the first time of the day. A feeling of excitement crept up his body. She had certainly dressed up for the evening. What a pretty necklace!

'Hi,' he said, 'I realized last night that I didn't even know your name. I'm Alan.'

'I'm Julie. I wondered whether you'd be here tonight as you weren't on the train this morning. Did you miss it?'

'No, I caught an earlier one as I had an important breakfast meeting. Shall we go? I thought you might like to try this new Italian restaurant I've found, unless you'd like to go somewhere else.'

'Is it far? I can't walk a long way in these heels.'

He looked at the very high heeled pink shoes. No, they were not good for walking.

'It's just five minutes down that road over there,' he said, pointing the way.

The evening went well and there were no pauses in the conversation. She tried to tell him what to choose from the menu, but he smiled and ordered something different. There was no point in having an argument about something so trivial. The food was good and they shared a bottle or two of wine.

'I'm paying half,' Julie said at the end of the meal. 'I hate women who don't pay their way.'

'Why not pay it all then?' he said. 'I really won't be offended.'

Julie laughed, 'You're so funny.'

As they walked back to the station she slipped her hand in his.

'Hey take your gloves off. It's no fun holding hands with a glove.'

'I promise I will as soon as we're settled somewhere quiet and comfy on the train. C'mon let's get going and we'll catch the nine-twenty.'

Just as they went through onto the platform he felt his hat come off his head and Julie planted a big kiss on his mouth. There was bold and there was brash and he realized he felt quite irritated by her behaviour. He looked up and round to see if anyone was watching and then firmly took back his hat and put it on his head.

'Let's just get on the train shall we? I'm sure we can find a quiet spot,' he said.

The last but one carriage was nearly empty, so he led the way to the far end and settled down in the corner seat. Julie immediately came and sat on him and removed his hat again. She started kissing him.

'I'm just going to pop to the loo,' he said. 'I'll be back in a sec.' He lifted her onto the adjacent seat and stood up. She flopped down and pouted her lips.

'Don't be long, lover,' she cooed.

He bent down to kiss her. His leather gloved hands caressed her long slim neck and suddenly he felt alive. The passion within her subsided as he became aroused. The train started to move. He stayed with her, enjoyed her company, more than any other part of the evening. She had stopped jabbering on. The calming sound of the train's engine was bliss. Why did women just keep on talking when they had nothing important to say?

When the train reached the stop before his usual stop he decided to get off. A little walk in the night air would do him good.

'Bye Julie,' he called over his shoulder as he stepped onto the platform. She had several stops to go yet, sitting neatly under her coat with her train ticket in her hand.

The air was cold and he walked briskly home. It had been a wonderful day after all. Julie had turned out to be quite enjoyable. He patted his briefcase unconsciously, as he held it in his arms across his chest. Now he must get moving and get home before his mother.

The house was in blackness as he arrived. He slipped straight down to the basement and took off his outer garments. Carefully shutting the door he went into the living room and switched the lights and TV on. By the time his mother got in he was lying on the sofa with a half drunk mug of tea by his feet.

'Hi son, have you been out?'

'No. Did you have a nice time at Betty's?'

'Same old, same old. She's getting doddery you know. Get us a cuppa. It's really cold out there.'

'You could get your own, you're still standing up.'

His mother sat down. 'Not now am I? Go on. You're out all day. You can look after me a bit in the evenings.'

He knew there was no point in arguing. No-one won arguments with his mother.

***

The next day they were sitting at the dining room table having breakfast when there was a banging on the door. He knew who that would be. He was wearing trousers that were a little too short for him and white socks inside carpet slippers. His hair was flattened and with a parting on the left and his brown knitted cardigan hung loosely. Dressing simply seemed to please his mother. Looking far from the sophisticated man about town he had looked yesterday he went to answer the door.

The police introduced themselves and asked to come in. He took them through to the kitchen.

'Oh no, not you lot again. What d'you want? He's not here and he's not been back.'

'Sorry Mrs Stephens but you know we have to check. I'm afraid there's been another murder. A young woman. Mind if we look around?'

'Yes I do. Why don't you leave us alone? All the neighbours will be out gawping through their net curtains.'

'Mother, the sooner they look, the sooner they'll be gone.'

'Oh you're so weak, not like your father; now he's a real man. Go ahead then plods – have your look. You won't find him 'cos he's not here.'

How he hated the plod. They snooped but not as closely as his mother because they weren't looking for secrets. They were looking for his father. Once they'd checked all the rooms they'd be gone.

'Can we just check the cellar, sir?' the young police woman asked. He felt faint, but before he'd time to think, his mother intervened.

'There ain't no cellar here missy. Now why don't you all just clear off?'

The police woman looked as if she was about to argue the point, but Sergeant Jones turned to her and said, 'There's no cellars in these houses. Come along Bates.' Then he turned to Mrs. Stephens, 'Thank you for your cooperation. It is appreciated. We'll be on our way.'

Alan showed them to the door.

He waited until later in the morning to slip unnoticed into the cellar and opened the cupboard door. He picked up the very high heeled pink shoes and stroked their shiny surface. They were beautiful. He remembered her long slim white throat against his fine, brown leather gloves. He remembered those moments when all her talking stopped and he could only hear the rhythmic sound of the train. How he wished his mother would shut up just like she had. He was tired of her constant nagging and moaning. He was tired of waiting on her. It was ironic that the father who had blighted his life was now taking the blame for his deeds.

He placed the shoes neatly on the shelf and lined them up exactly with the other four pairs. His collection was growing.

***

That evening there was a loud banging on the front door. Alan looked at his mother. What could they want now? Sergeant Jones and P.C. Bates stood at the front door, with other officers at the back of the house.

'This is police harassment,' screeched Mrs Stephens. 'Why don't you leave us alone?'

Sergeant Jones ignored her and turned to Alan. 'Can you tell me where you were on Friday evening?'

'He was with me,' replied Mrs Stephens. 'We spent the evening watching T.V.'

'Mr Stephens?'

'Yes, I was home with mother.'

'I am now going to arrest you on suspicion of murdering Julie Black. We have you on CCTV with Julie, getting onto the train on which she was found. When she took your hat off, you looked upwards and the camera caught a clear image. Bates give him his caution.' Then he turned to Mrs Stephens, 'You can come too. I'm charging you with obstructing a murder enquiry.'

Ghost Words

The meal on the table was full of colour. The smell of roast beef wafted across the room. Yorkshire puddings and roast potatoes were piled high and steam rose from dishes of sprouts, parsnips and carrots.

'Come on, you guys, settle down. Let's enjoy our lunch,' Derek said. 'I love our weekly get togethers. It's the only chance I get to play chef these days.'

'This looks great,' said Albert. 'It's such a treat after a busy week.'

'It sure is, Derek, you've done us proud as usual,' said Gerald.

'Well I love seeing you both,' he smiled at them as he started carving the meat. 'Help yourselves to vegetables.'

Gerald picked up the wine bottle and poured the drinks.

'Hey, I've some fantastic news. I've finally managed to get an exhibition for my work at Pritchard's Gallery. It starts on the 16th of next month. I hope you'll both be there.'

'That's great. You deserve to have your work recognised,' said Derek. 'Of course I'll be there.'

'Yes, well done. I'll certainly try to make it, but I have some important clients from Japan coming over that week,' said Albert.

'Oh thanks mate. Put your work first.' said Gerald.

'Now, now, I'm sure Albert will make it along to the gallery that week, even if he can't make it for the opening. So how many exhibits will you have?'

The brothers chatted on amiably. Derek heaped his plate with a second helping, while Albert fetched a jug of water and Gerald helped himself to more wine.

'Don't you get lonely here in this big house now you're on your own?' asked Albert.

'Well of course I miss mum, but it's nearly two years. No I'm fine.'

'It's just if you ever want some company you could come and stay with me. You'd have been welcome when Cara was with me but now I'm on my own, you'd be more than welcome.'

'Or you could stay at my place. There's more room at mine, but of course it's not as smart,' said Gerald.

'I'm fine here, unless of course you want to sell it. I do understand that your shares are tied up in my home.'

'Don't be daft,' Albert and Gerald said together.

Derek served up apple crumble and custard for pudding. It looked delicious so his brothers had a small portion although really they were full. Then they settled down on the sofas with coffee.

'What about coming to the gym with me, sometime Derek? said Albert.

'Oh give him a break Bert. We're not all fitness freaks,' said Gerald. 'You've got to learn to chill out Bert.'

'I do chill out. I enjoy Sundays with my brothers,' said Albert.

'And we enjoy Sundays with you,' replied Derek. 'I'd love to go to the gym sometime but I'll go for a swim. I don't fancy all those machines.'

'What about me? Are you going to invite me to your expensive gym?' asked Gerald.

'I wouldn't have thought you'd be interested. You're always too busy on some art project or chasing the girls,' replied Albert.

'Why don't you invite us both on the same day? It'll be fun all going together,' suggested Derek.

***

The following week they were all gathered round for another feast when suddenly Derek grabbed his chest and screamed with pain.

Albert shouted at Gerald, 'Call an ambulance,' as he tried to help Derek, but there was nothing to be done. Still in his thirties Derek died and Albert and Gerald were left with each other as the only remaining family.

As the weeks passed they had to arrange the funeral and decide what to do with the house.

'It's not the place I want to live,' said Albert, 'I think we should sell.'

'But it's our family home. I think we should keep it.'

'If you want to live here, that's fine.'

'I don't. You're the eldest, you should live here.'

Suddenly Gerald heard Derek's calming voice in his head. *Come on, you guys, settle down.* He looked round the old house. It was tired and cold. In that moment he realized that the warmth and the welcoming atmosphere of the house had come from Derek, not from bricks and mortar.

'Sorry Bert. Of course we should sell.'

After the house was sold, the two brothers drifted apart. In their own ways they both grieved for Derek. He had been their cement. He had smoothed over their differences. There were no more weekly dinners and few phone calls.

Albert remained busy in the city with his work, but one day he picked up a newspaper and he saw a picture of Gerald at the opening of his latest art exhibition. Gerald had not even told him about it. He put on his smart cashmere coat and made his way across London to the gallery. As he entered through the glass door he heard Derek's voice in his head, *I'm sure Albert will make it along to the gallery.*

He realized Derek had been telling them all along that they needed to keep in touch. He turned the corner and there was Derek looking straight at him from a large canvass; unselfish Derek, who looked after their mother and then looked after them.

He whipped a handkerchief out of his pocket to catch the tear as it slipped down his cheek and felt a strong arm come round his shoulder. It was Gerald.

'I miss him too. I'm so glad you came.'

'You're very talented Gerald. I always thought being an artist was a waste of time, but I was wrong. Derek saw your gift.'

'And I always thought you were totally obsessed by work, but you came today. Derek saw your kindness. I wish he was here today.'

They both stood in front of Derek's picture. The gallery was quiet and then a gentle voice said, *'Of course I'm here. Wouldn't miss seeing you two for the world.'*

An Error of Judgement

June smoothed down her skirt and propped her portfolio up against the side of her chair.

'Mr. Castle will see you now, Miss Spring,' said the secretary.

June took a deep breath and made her way into the modern office.

'Good morning Mr. Castle,' she said holding out her hand.

Mr Castle was already on his feet. The warm smile she glimpsed on his face disappeared as he looked at her. His skin whitened and eyes hardened, but he took her hand and gave a firm handshake.

'Please take a seat Miss Spring,' he said and then turned to face the panoramic window and raised his shoulders slowly. Within seconds he turned back to face her and took his seat.

'I've bought some of my work for you to look at,' June said to break the silence.

'I believe we've met before, but I doubt you remember.'

She looked at his dark face, the deep brown eyes that seemed to be glittering black at the moment. She would remember such a dynamic face.

'No, we haven't met.'

'Tell me Miss Spring, what were you doing yesterday evening?'

'I beg your pardon, but what has that to do with this meeting?'

'It was when we met. You bumped into me, literally and spilled your drink down my suit and when I said, Damn it woman, you're drunk, you said that you'd be sober in the morning but I'd still be a miserable old...'

'I was visiting my mother yesterday evening. She's broken her foot and I was helping her with a few little jobs.'

'I don't think I want a liar working for my company.'

June stood up, picking up her portfolio, 'And I would not want to work for someone who was so ignorant, but I would point out that it was you who telephoned me. It was you who requested this meeting and you have wasted my time and the cost of travelling down from Manchester.'

'See my secretary and she will reimburse you.'

June marched out of the room and straight past the secretary's office. 'What was all that about?' she thought taking her mobile out of her pocket.

'Hi Sis, my meeting was much shorter than I expected. Can we meet for lunch?' June said.

Soon they were sitting in a spacious Italian restaurant just round the corner from the advertising offices; enjoying a light lunch and a glass of chilled white wine when suddenly a shadow fell across their table.

They both looked up. Her sister Rose said, 'I know you. You bumped into me last night and were incredibly rude.'

Mr Castle looked at one sister and then the other. 'Twins. I didn't think of that.' He turned to June and said, 'I think I owe you an apology.'

'We're not twins. I'm three years older than my sister. Now we are enjoying a private lunch, if you don't mind.'

'Of course. I'm very sorry. Perhaps I could ring you?'

He walked off with his colleague to the back of the restaurant and June and Rose started to exchange notes about their encounters with Isaac Castle.

After lunch June spent a couple of hours with her mum and then took the train from Euston to Manchester. The trip had not turned out as she had wished. As an artist she didn't really want to work for an advertising agency but the offer had been such a good one. It would have allowed her to move back to London and be nearer her family. He really was a pig that man. Even if it had been her who'd had too much to drink and not her sister, what happened outside work shouldn't have influenced the interview.

Her mobile rang. Several people in the carriage looked over in her direction.

'Isaac Castle here. Miss Spring, I just wanted to say that I obviously made a mistake this morning and I'm sorry. I wondered if I could take you out for a meal this evening and we could discuss the job I was offering.'

'Anyone can make a mistake, Mr Castle, but you didn't listen to me when I told you where I was. I don't appreciate you calling me a liar.'

'Let me make it up to you. Could we meet tonight?'

'I'm on a train to Manchester as we speak. Anyway thank you for the apology, but I've decided that I'd rather carry on as I am and work independently.'

'Goodbye then Miss Spring.'

As she put her phone away she thought how the shape of his body had stood out against the bright light of his office window. Rose had said he was an arrogant sod, but as good looking as the devil and

June realized that she was absurdly disappointed not to be spending the evening with him.

She returned to her tiny studio in Manchester and threw herself into her work. Over the next months she produced a number of new works of art and managed to secure a month's exhibition in a small gallery on Oxford Road, near the BBC building.

On the evening of the opening June dressed in a floaty aquamarine dress, and her red curls tumbled down her back. Sometimes she tried to look businesslike but tonight she would look 'arty'. She wished her sister and mum were coming to see the exhibition tonight instead of next week. She needed their support. As it turned out she needn't have worried about being left with no-one to talk to, as the place was buzzing with people, many of whom wanted to ask her questions. June was amazed at the positive response to her work. Suddenly she looked across the room and there was Isaac Castle standing by one of her paintings. She had thought about him frequently in the last months, wondering what might have been if her sister hadn't been celebrating her friend's hen party that night.

He stood tall and straight examining the picture in front of him. Would he recognise himself in the painting he was looking at?

June picked up a second glass of Champagne and walked over to him.

'Good evening. I'm surprised to see you here, Mr Castle.'

He smiled, 'Isaac, please.'

She handed him the drink. 'Is there anything you've seen that you like?'

'Oh plenty. The evening is going well. You've been very busy.'

'Yes, lots of people come on a first night. Are you up here on business?'

'No,' he paused, 'I saw your exhibition advertised and I wanted to see more of your work. I like lots of your pictures but this one would go very well in my office.'

June blushed. 'Yes the view from your window is inspirational.'

'Can I take you for a drink when you've finished here?'

She paused. It would be silly to say no, when he obviously liked her work and had come so far to see it. 'I'll be finished in half an hour. That'd be lovely.'

They went for a drink in a spacious hotel bar. Although there were plenty of people around they seemed far away.

'Will you be coming down to London soon, to visit your family?'

'No they're coming up here next week. I shan't be down until the exhibition is over.'

'Well when you do come down, will you come out for a meal?'

'Are you asking me out? I thought it was my art you were interested in.'

'It was at first, but I was fascinated at the style you showed waking out of my office and then dismissing me with a curt sentence in the restaurant. Somehow you keep springing up in my head. So to answer my question was that a yes?'

June laughed, 'It's a definite maybe.'

They walked back to her flat in the quiet of late evening. He took her hand and she felt unbelievably aware of his warm strong fingers linked with her own. It was good that he could not see her burning face in the darkness.

When they arrived she said, 'I won't invite you in for a coffee as we've only just met really, but I will call when I come to London.'

She stood on tiptoe to give him a kiss on the cheek but he moved so that their lips met; first gently, but then more passionately and she found her arms had somehow round wound his neck. Her heart was thumping. What was it about this man that she was so drawn to? Whatever it was she did not want the evening to end.

'Coffee?' she said.

'Yes. No sugar.' He said as they walked up the path. 'And no milk,' he said as she put the key in the door.

June led him into the small lounge.

'And no coffee,' he said as he leant down to kiss her.

'Cheeky,' she replied, but there the conversation ended.

The Pigeon Fancier

Dan hurried home from work, nodded to his wife and headed to the pigeon loft.

'I've had enough,' screamed Marge. 'It's them bleeding birds or me. Make your mind up. You spend more time with 'em than me.'

'Now, now Marge, when I get down from giving them their grits and corn, we'll 'ave a proper talk and see what can be done to make you happy,' Dan said. 'You get the dinner on and I'll be down in half an hour.'

Up in the loft he stretched his arms and breathed a sigh of relief. 'Ah, Bessie, there's me girl. Had a good flight my darling. Brushed off the cobwebs, ready for tomorrow's race.'

Of course Dan loved all his pigeons but Bessie was his out and out favourite and so was her mother before her. An hour and a half later, Dan descended the stairs to find the house in darkness.

What was Marge playing at? he thought as he switched on the light. The silence hit him. The usual noise of the television wasn't assaulting his ears. Nor was Marge's plaintive voice. He saw the note propped up by the clock. He knew what it would contain; more threats of leaving.

He went over to the cooker and checked to see if she'd left his dinner, but it was cold and empty. He looked in the fridge but there was only a limp lettuce leaf. The freezer wasn't any better with just a litre of milk and some chocolate ice cream. 'Bloody woman,' he thought. 'Still fish and chips would do.' Then when he'd eaten, he'd think what to do about Marge.

Later as he sat with his feet on the coffee table, eating his meal out of newspaper, he enjoyed the quiet. Marge could nag for Britain. She certainly wouldn't approve of his eating dinner, with his feet up. Then he thought of Bessie and her gentle song. She worked her heart out for him, flying hundreds of miles and always coming back to him; Bessie, who always greeted him with warmth.

His mind wandered to Marge, who was increasingly cross with him these days; Marge, who needed him to go chasing across the town, to declare his undying love. He opened the note she'd left him.

IF THOSE BLOODY BIRDS AREN'T GONE BY TOMORROW THEN I WILL BE GONE FOREVER.

Oh dear, she was serious. I suppose I should do something, Dan thought.

He went upstairs and packed a bag. He needed to hurry. There was little time. He rushed across town to his wife.

Two hours later, he was back home in bed. Marge had been right. It had been the time to make a choice and so he'd taken her some clothes. Tomorrow he needed to be up at five for Bessie. It was her best race and she'd been working hard training for it. He had to get her to Portsmouth by seven.

Unexpected

'I think we should call the police,' said Gemma. 'Mum's never been this late home before. Something might've happened to her.'

'We'll give her another hour and if she's not home then, I'll give them a ring,' said Alan. 'Why don't you go to bed love? There's no point in two of us waiting up.'

'Dad I just can't. I'm worried about her. She's never this late. She's not answering her phone. What's the point of waiting?'

'Because...'

'Because what?' said Gemma.

Alan sighed and Gemma noticed how tired he looked. 'Because I think your mum may be having an affair. Maybe she's forgotten the time.'

'Mum wouldn't do that. You're wrong. How could you even think that? I'm going to listen to music in my room but I'll be down in an hour,' Gemma said as she slammed the door. Something was wrong. She could feel it. As she went past her parents' room she looked through the open door. There on the bed was her mum's phone. She slipped into the room and picked it up. Well that explained why she'd not been answering it.

She entered her mum's password and went into her own room to read the messages. If her mum was having an affair there would be evidence here. Sitting on the edge of her bed she scanned the messages, but there was nothing in the inbox. Then she looked in deleted messages and there were fifty or so messages from Gerald. Who was Gerald? For the first time she realized her mum had a life that she'd kept secret. Gemma felt betrayed. She'd thought she and her mum were close.

Knowing that she shouldn't read the messages she put the phone down and looked at it as it lay on the bed beside her. She picked it up again almost immediately. Her mum could still be in trouble. She opened the last message from Gerald.

Alice, I liked the dress you wore today. Perhaps it should be a bit shorter. Xoxo

Thinking that was a strange message, she opened another one.

I saw you drop your daughter off at St Thomas's School. Pretty, but not a patch on you.

Gemma felt the room chill and realized her hand was shaking. She scrolled down to sent messages and looked for Gerald's name. There was only one.

I'm married Gerald and I have no wish to go out with you. I'm sure there's someone special for you just around the corner.

Her mother was being stalked. She dialled the police and told them everything she'd found out and then ran downstairs to tell her dad.

Within ten minutes Inspector Carr and Sergeant Sampson arrived in a car driven by a police constable. Gemma showed them into the kitchen, where her dad was perched on a stool. He got up, wiped his hand down his trousers and shook hands with the officers.

'Can you tell me when you last saw your wife Mr Waterford?' said Sergeant Sampson, while Inspector Carr wandered around the room looking at everything.

'She left at five to go to work. We were expecting her home at 9.30.'

'Mum's never later than ten,' said Gemma.

'And where's her phone now?'

Gemma handed it over and Sergeant Sampson placed it carefully into an evidence bag.

'Aren't you going to read the messages?' asked Gemma.

'We certainly are but it's important that we fingerprint it first,' said Sergeant Carr.

'But it'll be mine on it. I've read some of the messages.'

'Don't worry, Miss Waterford. We'll sort it all out. We will need your fingerprints for elimination.'

The police officers took down details of Mrs Waterford's car and place of work. They seemed to ask endless questions and Gemma was wondering if they'd ever start looking for her mother. Inspector Carr casually sat down by the computer and asked if this was the one that Mrs Waterford uses. She then started tinkering with the keys and soon had Alice's private e-mails up on display. Hitting the deleted box, Inspector Carr found over two hundred emails from Gerald.

'Do either of you know any Gerald, perhaps from her work?' she asked.

'No, she's never mentioned him,' said Gemma.

'No,' said Alan.

'Well he's obviously being a real pain and she's doing the right thing by not engaging in conversation with him. Very strange that she never told you about this,' said Inspector Carr to Alan.

'Well she didn't,' said Alan.

'Gemma, will you show me your mother's bedroom?'

'She doesn't have a bedroom. We share,' said Alan.

'Sorry sir, just a matter of speech. Gemma could you show me your parents' room?' Gemma started to lead the way upstairs, when Inspector Carr's phoned rang.

After a short conversation she said, 'Yes we'll be right there.'

'We think we've found her car, Gemma. I need to go, but I'll be back.'

'I'll come too. I can tell you if anything's different about it. I promise not to get in the way,' she said and then whispered, 'and I need to talk to you.'

Inspector Carr popped her head round the kitchen door, 'Sir, we're taking your daughter with us to identify the car. We should be back within the hour. I'm leaving PC Thomson with you in case she comes back.'

They had just got in the car when Carr's phone went again. 'OK, don't let him go. I'll be right there.'

She closed her phone and asked Gemma what she had to tell her.

'It's just that mum doesn't ever tell dad anything. He's a bit of a control freak, which is probably why she didn't let on about Gerald making a complete pest of himself. Dad would've thought there was something in it.'

'Right Gemma, we're just popping into the station, before we go and look at the car. I'm going to ask you to wait for me. I promise not to be long.'

Gemma was taken to the near empty canteen where a tired looking policeman bought her a cup of tea and took her to a seat in the corner. She was left there on her own with nothing to do but imagine what was going on. Minutes passed and then more minutes. It was just coming up to an hour when in came Inspector Carr and Sergeant Sampson.

'There's been some developments. You can come with us if you promise to stay in the car.'

'Yes, of course.' Gemma stood up and hurried out of the canteen.

'When we got back to the station there was a man named Gerald Toynton waiting for us. He works at the care home where your mother works. Toynton's still in the police station, while we check his story. Ever heard the name?'

Gemma shook her head.

'He admits to following your mother. He thinks she's in love with him and she's tied into this awful marriage. Your mother left the house at five and he was just about to follow, when a man came out of the house, got into a large blue estate and took off after her. Gerald says then he followed.'

'Dad's car's a blue estate, but I don't think he went out. I suppose he could've done as I'd just started dying my hair when mum left.'

'Right, well anyway the blue car started flashing your mum's car, just in the lane by the railway line. Then the man got out and so did your mother and he dragged her across the fields. Gerald says he stayed in the car because he was frightened. We'll know in any case because if he was there there'll be DNA. About five minutes later the man came back to his car without your mother.'

'So did Gerald go and look or what?' said Gemma.

''Fraid not, he went and drank a lot of whisky, but then he came to see us. Ah here we are. Now I want you to stay with the ambulance people, while we go and look.'

Gemma looked around her and a distant memory came flashing back. 'There's an old shed under the railway bridge. He used to take me there as a child.'

Inspector Carr strode off with a number of officers shouting out orders.

Gemma was pacing up and down. 'What if they couldn't find her?' Her heart was beating quickly. Then from a distance she heard a shout.

'Bring the stretcher. Over here. She's still breathing.'

The two medics were off across the field and soon her mother was in the ambulance, tearing along the roads to hospital with Gemma and Sergeant Sampson squashed in the back.

Alice Waterford lay sedated at the hospital with Gemma sitting beside her in the chair. Sergeant Sampson was keeping her company so he could take a statement when Alice woke up. They had drunk several cups of dishwater tea from small plastic cups when Inspector Carr put her head round the door.

She spoke quietly. 'I'm afraid P.C. Thompson's in A&E with concussion. Your dad's fled. Not to worry 'cos someone will stay with your mum all night, but I don't think he'll be back.'

Gemma's mind was whizzing with so many thoughts. 'How had her dad got away? Where would he have gone? Would P.C. Thompson be alright?'

'You'll have to keep an eye on your mum, lass,' said Sergeant Sampson. She seems to attract some very dubious men.'

'Sergeant, remember one of them is Gemma's father,' said Inspector Carr. 'Actually it's all very weird, but if Alice Waterford hadn't been being stalked she might've been dead when we found her. It's the first time I've known a stalker save the day.'

The Sting

Katie slipped her sandals off and ran along the beach. She could feel wet sand on her feet and smell the freshness of the sea. There was no one about. She listened to the sound of the waves gently tapping the shore.

She needed time to herself to think. Alan her boyfriend for five years, had just dumped her. Obviously she was upset; she must be – five years was a long time. It was just that she didn't actually feel upset, in fact she felt positively relieved. There would be no more rushing around to please him. He would never have allowed her to walk along the beach just to enjoy the fresh air. He'd have found her little tasks like ironing his shirts or cleaning his shoes.

She walked at the edge of the water until she'd almost reached the end of the cove. A few people were beginning to appear, but it was still peaceful. The sun cast a golden glow on the water. It was beautiful. Suddenly a sharp pain shot through her foot. Looking down she saw a purple blue jellyfish, which seemed to be panting. Hobbling to the wooden breakwater she sat down almost crying with the excruciating pain.

A young man, followed by a black and white Collie, came running towards her.

'Are you hurt?' he called.

'Yes I've been stung by a jellyfish, although it feels like I've been stabbed.'

'Was it a blue one with purple splodges?' he asked. She nodded.

'Hmmmm they can be a bit nasty. We don't usually get those here, but I noticed a few yesterday. I'm going to take you to the hospital.'

Within seconds strong arms had scooped her up and she could feel the warmth of him as he carried her to his car.

'By the way, I'm Steve.'

'Katie,' she replied.

Her foot throbbed. She vaguely thought about being alone in a car with a stranger. That wasn't very sensible, but she could feel herself sweating and cold at the same time. The dog, Patch looked at her with interest, but she couldn't respond.

By the time they reached A & E her foot had swollen and she was feeling faint. Steve spoke to the triage nurse and she was taken straight to the doctor who gave her a steroid jab. While she rested in the narrow bed Steve kept her company, popping out to the car now and again to check that Patch was alright. When the swelling eased a little, Katie was allowed to go home. The danger of a further reaction had passed.

As they approached Steve's car he smiled at her and said, 'Did I save your life? Does that get me a date?'

She looked at him and took in what an attractive man he was. Sitting in the car she realized she hadn't looked at another man for a long time.

But it was Patch who took the first kiss by giving Katie a big lick on her face.

The Last Wish

Pippa strode uphill, with her blond hair streaming out behind her. She kept walking, choosing which way to go without thinking. Her thoughts were charging round her head as her feet pounded the pavement. 'What should she do about Nick?'

She'd spent the morning, cleaning her Grandmother's flat. Her gran really needed some professional help but she didn't like strangers in her home, so every Saturday morning Pippa, cleaned the flat and did the week's shopping. She willingly spent time there as she loved her Gran but she'd rather have been chatting to her than cleaning the oven. At eleven she would stop for coffee, so that they had a little time to talk. 'But Gran needs more frequent help,' thought Pippa 'and how am I going to manage that and keep on top of my job?'

'And what about Nick? Why does he want to get married when we've only known each other a month? What's it all about?' She walked further than she'd walked before and suddenly she realized that she had no idea where she was. She stopped and took a water bottle from her bag and had a sip. There were no pavements anymore; she'd walked right out of the town and into the country. It was beautiful. The greenness of it all hit her, so deep and rich and then she saw the flowers; mauves, pinks, blues were shivering on fragile stems in the slight breeze. Behind them was a tiny cottage. She would go and ask the owner the way back to the seafront and with that positive thought she walked through the creaky gate and banged on the door knocker. It was tarnished, probably brass, and almost black. She pulled down the sleeve of her jumper so that it covered the heel of her palm and rubbed the knocker, until a hint of gold shone through.

Suddenly the door swung open, 'So what do you want? I was having a sleep, you impatient girl.'

'Oh I'm so sorry to have disturbed your nap, but I only knocked once.'

'You kept on rubbing, that's what woke me. Now what's it you want?'

'Just some directions to the seafront. I'm a bit lost.'

The old woman raised her eyes to the sky. Pippa noticed that the woman's hair fell in charcoal waves about the richly coloured layers of silk and chiffon that the old lady wore. She should have looked odd but there was a strange completeness in the old lady. She just looked right. Her skin was so wrinkly there was hardly a smooth part on her.

'Good grief girl, you've no idea what you've done. I should be retired. Not just having rests. I should've stopped work centuries ago. Yes I am as old as the hills. Now it seems to me if you kept taking the highest road to get up here, then you need to take the lowest roads to get down to the sea.'

'Oh thank you. Now you've said that, it's so obvious. I'm very sorry I've disturbed you,' Pippa said as she turned to leave.

'It doesn't work like that, lady. You have to stay and tell me the three things you want most in the world. Then you can go and I can get on and then back to sleep.'

Pippa realized the old lady must be lonely, so she turned back, prepared to humour her.

'I'd like my Gran to accept a carer to come into her home to help her as I'm going to struggle as she needs more care,' said Pippa.

'I don't need your life history, girl. Wish one – a home help for Pippa's Gran. Next!' snapped the old lady.

'I'd like everyone in the world to be happy.'

'Oh dear!' sneered the woman. 'Wish two – everyone happy.'

Pippa ignored the woman's rudeness. She was obviously under some stress.

'C'mon, I'm not waiting all day. Wish three.'

'I'd like you to be able to retire,' said Pippa.

All the wrinkles on the woman's face lifted and she gave Pippa a broad smile.

'Well I never! Well I never. Work to do.' She went to close the door and then swung it open again, 'See you tomorrow,' and the door slammed shut.

'But why would I see you tomorrow? What a strange lady,' thought Pippa.

Pippa went out through the gate and started her long walk home. When she arrived at her flat there were two messages on the answerphone. She pressed the button.

'Hi Pippa. Just wanted to ask you round for a meal tonight and bring that new boyfriend of yours,' said her dad.

The second message was from Nick. 'I thought I'd pop round at seven this evening. Hope you've got good news for me.'

Pippa felt slightly irritated at Nick's continual pressure. She went into the bathroom to shower and change.

When she and Nick arrived at her Dad's place they were given a drink.

'So this is your new young man,' her dad said.

'Hoping to get married very soon,' said Nick.

Her Dad smiled. Nick looked around the large room which was exquisitely decorated and had several large paintings on the wall. Pippa felt awkward. She didn't want to contradict Nick but she really hadn't made up her mind about this marriage. They all went into dinner. Pippa and Nick sat opposite her two sisters, Samantha and Sarah. Her dad sat at the head of the table.

'I've a great idea for your Gran,' said Sarah. 'Wendy from college is looking for a little job. You can take her round to your Gran and then see if she could do some of the care for her. What d'you think?'

'Oh Wendy's lovely. I think that might just work,' Pippa replied.

'Tell me, why do you say, 'your Gran'? Isn't she your Gran as well?' Nick addressed Sarah.

'Well technically she's not my Gran, although we all love her. She's Pippa's Gran. Dad's Pippa's step father.'

'Oh, you never said,' Nick turned towards Pippa.

'I never thought about it.'

'I've brought Pippa up since she was three and she's as much my daughter as these two. Tell me something Nick, when you have children how will you bring them up?'

'I'll do everything I can to help them. I'll get them the best education, support them through college and buy them a house when they're older. I want to be a good dad.'

'And so do I. All my children have gone to a good state school. They've worked or are working their way through college and I'll help Sam and Sarah with a deposit for their first home, as I did for Pippa. Then they're on their own. Of course there'll always be a home here for them if they ever need it, but I want them to be responsible adults.'

Pippa looked across at Nick. She saw disappointment in his eyes and suddenly knew why he'd been so interested. What a fool she'd been. He'd thought she was going to be rich. She knew it was over now. Pippa looked across at her dad and smiled. She knew he'd seen through Nick within minutes. That's why he was such an astute businessman. They made polite conversation through the rest of the meal and then Pippa made an excuse to go home.

Arriving home she slumped onto the sofa and switched on the television. The news was showing a dreadful earthquake in China. Suddenly Pippa was fully alert again. 'What had she done?' she thought.

A woman covered in dirt was being interviewed. 'I'm so happy. My husband and three children are missing, but it's been an amazing day. That pile of stones there used to be my house. Look at it now. Can you believe how powerful the Earth is?' The woman gave a broad smile.

The next news item was a father being interviewed having caused a pile up on the M42. 'Well I can't really take any blame as I fell asleep at the wheel. You can't be accountable when you're unconscious. Anyway I'll have a nice rest in prison and that's what I need. Been working too hard lately.' He grinned at the camera.

She flicked channels to find a singer paying a tribute to Wayne Taylor, the eighties icon, who'd died suddenly. 'It's great he's dead. I'm so happy for him. It'll make his sales go up now.'

Pippa knew now why the old lady had said she would see her tomorrow. She must get the happiness wish cancelled. She laughed at herself. Who'd have thought she would've believed in a magic brass knocker and an old woman giving out three wishes. The world had gone mad.

At six o'clock Pippa was up and dressed with walking shoes and a bottle of water. Up the hill she trudged. The air was nippy but fresh. It was a beautiful morning. On an on she went until the little cottage came into view.

Pippa went through the creaking gate to see that the place was derelict. The windows were boarded up and the brass knocker had gone. She noticed a small envelope pinned to the door and read the note inside.

Pippa,
You gave me the one thing I've waited for; my freedom after 2000 years. It seems such a lovely job to give people wishes, but it became a curse. All those years listening to greedy people who wanted eternal life and piles of treasure, but you wanted good things for other people. I knew wish two would be a nightmare so, to thank you, I didn't grant it. I just cast a spell so you would see the consequences if I had. Instead I granted the wish you should have asked for, which was to see Nick's true colours. Your Gran should be fine with you and Wendy helping her and I'm sure there's happiness for you around the corner.
Ever Grateful
Jeannie

Pippa breathed a sigh of relief. At least the world would not be cursed with everyone being happy all the time. She went to put the letter into her pocket, but the wind tugged at it and it flew into the air.

Inherited

Kvanita glugged the milk straight from the bottle, blind to her surroundings. She hadn't realized how thirsty she was. The bottle was nearly empty when the shadow fell across her. She didn't have time to look up before her collar was grabbed and she was lifted almost off her feet.

'Well, what 'ave we got ourselves 'ere?' said a husky female voice.

Kvanita remained silent. She was too tired to fight. The woman twisted her round.

'You look like a runaway. Am I right?'

Kvanita nodded. Her eyes took in the large shabby Georgian house; the paint peeling from the rotten windows and a wooden shutter hanging from its hinge. And then the world went black.

When she woke up she was on a mattress on the floor of a room and a not too clean sleeping bag had been slung over her. There were strands of light coming through the holes in the curtain. It was warm and dry. She turned over and went back to sleep.

Some hours later she woke to find the old woman staring at her. 'I thought you were a gonna there for a minute. Thought you were never going to wake up. Everyone round here calls me Gran. There's a few young uns stopping with me and you can for a coupla nights. Come on love, I'll get you some food.'

Kvanita followed Gran down the uncarpeted stairs into a warm kitchen. There was a giant pan of stew on the stove and a large table in the room, covered with a floral plastic cloth.

'Best get that down you before the others get in.'

'Thank you. My name's Kvanita. Thanks so much for the sleep and food. I'm sorry I took the milk.'

'Don't worry 'bout it.'

She had just finished her bowl of food when three lads came in. They dumped their belongings on the end of the long wooden table, stared at Kvanita and then helped themselves to some stew.

'Hey Gran, I've got you some food. I whipped a trolley full, while someone was having their coffee. Then I had to saunter out the shop as if I'd been shopping. It was a right laugh.'

'Where's it now, Tyler?' asked Gran.

'Outside.'

'Then bring it in, you oaf, and go and get rid of the trolley,' said an older boy called Lucas.

Zac the oldest of them all unzipped his jacket and said, 'I've got your favourite Gran.' He placed a large bottle of gin on the table.

'How do you do that? How'd you get them to take the security tags off?' said Lucas.

Zac touched the side of his nose. 'It's a little trick the Gran taught me and she'll tell you when you're old enough.'

Kvanita watched in silence. It was like that musical she'd watched, with that horrible man in charge of an army of boys thieving. She knew right from wrong. She'd only taken the milk because the thirst had been terrible. Wisely she kept quiet.

'Come on Kvanita, you can help me put this stuff away,' said Gran.

'Why do they call you the Gran?' she asked.

'Well I am a gran but not necessarily theirs. I'm also head of this house so it shows some respect.'

The next day Kvanita came down to the kitchen at ten in the morning. She had a lot of sleep to catch up on and although the house was not ideal, she felt safe. The boys were gone and the Gran was having a large mug of coffee.

'There's some Rice Crispies in that cupboard,' said Gran.

Kvanita climbed on a chair to get down the packet and poured herself a glass of milk. She was still hungry but not in the painful way of yesterday.

'So, why've you run away from your mum?' asked Gran.

'Oh. I didn't. My mum died and my dad got lumbered with me. He says I'm a waste of space. I don't keep the house clean and when he's drunk he hits me so hard. I have to hide.' She lifted her T shirt and showed the Gran the bruises on her tiny body. 'I'm not always quick enough. Then in the morning he's back to shouting at me again. He hates me. I can't go back there.'

'And how old are you?' said Gran.

'Eight.'

'You're like the boys. All had a bad time, one way or another. You can stay here today, while I have a think. I've got a grandkid your age. Now go and play in the garden and give me a bit of space.'

It was later in the afternoon when Gran called her in. 'When you've had that sandwich you can help me peel some veg.'

'OK,' said Kvanita climbing up to the big table.

'The thing is we all pay our way in this little family. The boys are all a lot older than you so we don't have to worry about them being stopped for not going to school. As you saw yesterday they bring stuff home from the shops that we can use. Other stuff I sell and that pays the bills. If you want to stay I've thought of a way, but I'm not a charity case. You'll have to pay your way too.'

'I do want to stay, but I've never nicked things.'

'Oh we can teach you how. Don't worry 'bout that.'

And so Kvanita's alternative education began.

***

The first few days she just went out and followed the boys from a distance and watched them. She didn't really like what they did, but she liked the big house, the warm food and the lack of violence. The boys tolerated her, but she was too young to interest them. It was like having a real family.

Then she was given a task. She had to take an apple from a greengrocers. She followed Lucas in and watched as he pocketed a number of pieces of fruit. At the door he turned, stuck his tongue out at her and legged it.

'She's with him,' shouted the assistant.

The manager caught her arm. 'I'm not with him, honest,' she said. 'And I haven't taken anything. You can search me. I haven't.'

'I saw you two looking at each other,' said the assistant.

'I just thought he was nicking things, that's all; that's why I was looking,' said Kvanita and then burst into tears.

The manager looked at her. 'So what did you come in here for? You don't seem to have a purse.'

'I just wanted an apple for school,' she said unfolding her palm, which contained a pound coin. The manager glared at the assistant, picked up two apples and put them in a brown paper bag.

'You keep your money love, and enjoy these.'

Kvanita took the bag and left the shop. She'd learned two things. That she was going to be rubbish at stealing, but she was good at lying. She returned to the big house with her apples and the pound coin. They didn't know the apples had been a gift as she'd dumped the bag. She was now officially part of the family.

As the months passed Kvanita learned to improve her skills. She didn't like actually stealing but she was good at blagging money out of people. She'd lost her bus fair and didn't know if she could walk that far home. She'd dropped her mum's purse somewhere and she'd been sent to get milk for the baby. There were a lot of kind and generous people about. She also became used to people blanking her and pretending they couldn't hear her and sometimes they told her to get lost in no uncertain terms.

Then one day several years later she was sent to nick some cough medicine from the chemist for Zac, who was quite poorly. No-one would give her money that day, so she stuffed it down her jumper and a big hand grabbed her as she went to leave the shop. She tried crying. She tried lying but the security guard was having none of it.

'Surely you should be at school,' he said.

Kvanita remembered the story Gran had schooled her in. 'I live with my Gran and she home-schools me. My parents are living abroad. My cousin's ill and I dropped the money Gran gave me for his medicine. I've never done this before.'

'We always prosecute, love. Sit here.'

She could hear the guard and the manager discuss the matter, but not the actual words they said.

The security guard whipped out his phone and took a picture of her. Then he said, 'Alright love as it was medicine you were taking we'll let you take it home, but I have your picture and if you don't return with the money tomorrow I'll be calling the police. Understand?'

'Thank you, sir. I promise I'll be back tomorrow, first thing.'

When she told Gran the story she was not pleased. She put her coat on and marched Kvanita back to the shop.

'Here's the money for the cough mixture,' she said. 'I'm sorry my grandchild is such an idiot. She'll be punished, you mark my words.'

'Thank you for coming in so promptly Madam,' said the manager.

'There's just one other little thing,' said Gran. 'I'm not happy that the security guard should be taking photographs of young girls. I just don't feel comfortable about it.'

The manager called the man over and made him delete the photograph in front of Gran. She thanked the manager again and said she must get back to her sick grandson and they left.

'I'm sorry I caused so much trouble,' said Kvanita.

'Just don't get caught again and avoid that shop for a while. He'll not forget your face. Mark my words.'

Life went on as usual for several years but gradually the cousins realized that Gran did less. She needed help with making the meal and wasn't so pleased at getting items that she had to sell. Lucas started to find people he could flog things to and Kvanita helped out with the food. This meant she spent more time alone with her during the day.

One morning Kvanita went into the kitchen but Gran wasn't there. She made her a cup of tea and took it up to her room. The cousins never went into the Gran's room. It was out of bounds.

Kvanita knocked.

'Who is it?' Gran snapped.

'It's just me. I've bought you a cup of tea.'

'Well bring it in girl.'

It was a large room crammed with beautiful objects. The room defied the rest of the house, which was shabby, comfortable, but threadbare. Kvanita opened her eyes in wonder. The furnishings were rich. A flat screen TV hung on a wall and there were vases and jewellery on every surface. It was like an Aladdin's cave.

Kvanita placed the tea on the bedside table.

'Are you not feeling well?'

'I've been better. You'll have to do your work this morning and help with the food tonight. I'm having a day in bed.'

Kvanita did what she could to make the Gran comfortable and then went out to bring in her contribution to the family. Keeping the house going and nursing the Gran was hard work but Kvanita felt loyalty to the woman who had saved her from her violent father. The cousins also did what they could as they too knew that although the Gran had used them, she had also looked after them.

As time went by Gran's condition worsened and the cousins put up with Kvanita bringing in less, but not without some resentment. She felt they worried that she was becoming the Gran's favourite.

One morning when Kvanita took tea upstairs, Gran told her to sit down. 'I'm dying Kvanita and this house will go to Lucas. He really is my grandson. There'll be nothing for you child and I doubt if they'll want you to stay from what they've been saying. You've been a good girl, now go and make a life for yourself. You're old enough and bright enough.'

'Can't we get a doctor and get you well?'

'Nope, I've been there and there's no hope. However somewhere in this house I believe there's a very valuable vase and you should search for it and take it. They won't notice one item. It was stolen by my old man and was far too hot to flog at the time. I hid it somewhere but for the life of me can't remember where.'

'I don't want you to die,' said Kvanita.

Gran shook her head, 'Listen, the vase is silver. It's very old and has large rubies, emeralds and diamonds set into the top of it. You're a bright girl; start looking. I think you're going to need it.'

In between nursing the Gran and preparing food Kvanita knew it made sense to start searching. While the boys were out she went through the dusty attic, which was full of all sorts of bits and pieces. If they sold all those things on eBay they'd be rich.

It was a quiet group of four cousins who sat round the table that night. They'd all been there as Gran had taken her last breath. Kvanita couldn't help crying quietly and the boys had lost their lively banter.

Then Lucas spoke. 'Kvanita, I know you've looked after Gran as she did you, but you're not part of this family. You don't contribute enough. We're going to expand the business and you don't fit in. We've talked about it and we all want you out.' Lucas looked her straight in the eye, but Tyler and Zac had the grace to be studying the wood patterns of the table.

'Of course I'll go, but who'll cook for you?'

Lucas gave a shallow laugh. 'We never want to eat a bloody stew again.'

'Can I go tomorrow morning? I don't want to be looking for somewhere in the dark. I can go and sit in my room if you don't want me around.'

Lucas lent back in his chair. 'As long as you're gone by the time we get back in the evening, that'll be fine. I'll ring you when the funeral's arranged. You can come to that. Anyway we're going out for a drink now, so you don't have to stay in your room.'

They stood up and picked up keys and phones and made for the door. Tyler hung back a bit. 'There's a new squat behind the old cinema. They'll still have some room. Say you're a friend of mine,' he said and then pulled the door shut behind him. That'll be a good stand-by she thought, knowing that she'd already found a possible place where she could be on her own; not as comfortable as this house, that had been her home for eight years, but somewhere she could get by for a few weeks.

She loved this house. It was empty now and unusually quiet. The Gran lay peacefully upstairs. Kvanita took a deep breath and made herself get up. The search for the vase was on.

***

The next day Kvanita entered the cellar with trepidation. She could smell the dampness and mould. The stone steps were slimy. She lit her Maglite torch and flashed it around so that she could see where the steps ended and the floor began.

Moving some chairs stacked on an old table she started rummaging through the cupboards and drawers of the rotting furniture. She knew she hadn't got long. 'It must be here,' she thought. The Gran had said it was in the house and she'd searched everywhere else.

The vase she was looking for was small and old. It could be anywhere. If the cousins found her here there'd be trouble. She was just a girl and she could make money in other ways, they'd said. They'd always been mean to her but when the Gran had been alive there had been some protection.

Peering in the dim light, she heard a noise overhead. They were back. Hardly daring to breathe she continued her search, but how was she going to get out. Then she remembered that there was a trap door from the garden into the cellar. She flicked the torch about searching at the end of the cellar, where the ceiling dropped low, almost like an attic. There were the doors.

The noises were getting louder. They were coming her way. She pushed open one of the doors and as the light streamed in it fell on a black, rough object. 'That could be the vase,' she thought, stuffing it down her jumper and heaving herself outside into the fresh air. A bright beam of light splashed into the cellar from the kitchen door, just as she eased the trap door shut.

She ran as fast as she could. If they'd seen the light they would be after her. Her heart was beating fast. 'What would they do if they caught her?' she thought.

As she turned through the gate to freedom a hand grabbed her.

'I had a feeling you were about. Now what 'ave we got 'ere then? You suddenly up the duff or is that a piece of our property you've just taken,' said Zac, the oldest cousin.

Reluctantly she took the blackened vase out of her jumper.

'I just wanted a little memento to remember this place by. I know you boys don't want me here but it's

the only home I've had. Here take it. I won't be back.'
She held it out to him.

'You know what kid, you can 'ave it. I don't want it.
It's a piece of old junk. But make sure you don't come
back 'ere for anything else or you'll be in trouble with
Lucas. Understand?'

She took back the vase and murmured, 'Thanks.'
Then she made herself walk away as casual as she
had to when she was nicking from the shops. As she
turned the corner she broke into a run and ran like the
cops were after her. It was good that it had been Zac
who had caught her. He wasn't the brightest button in
the box, but the others might still come after her.

Kvanita stuffed the vase down her jumper and
made her way to the other side of the city, where
earlier she'd discovered an open garden shed in a
property that was up for sale. It was better than being
on the streets and would give her time to sort herself
out.

Life might not be perfect, but if she could work out
a way to sell the vase, probably by taking out the
jewels and flogging them one by one, she might make
enough to go straight. And with that thought she
started cleaning the vase with some old cloth she
found lying around the shed, humming a little tune to
herself, as the silver started to peek out from the
blackness.

The next day she decided to do some research
about the vase on the internet. She hid it in her bag
and walked through the town to her usual library
where she spent a lot of time. It was warm and the
librarians never minded her hanging around as she
often helped people use the computers. She waited
her turn to search the internet and soon found the

information she was looking for. The vase was four hundred years old and had been stolen from Highbury House. There was a small reward being offered. It was so wrong to break up something so old but what else could she do? She couldn't claim the reward because she had no address. She just had to accept there was no other choice. She put her hand into the bag and touched it. If only she had a job and a place to live she thought, then she could return the vase to the rightful owners.

'Hi Kvanita,' said one of the librarians. 'Don't suppose you want a temporary job for six weeks.'

'Hi Anne. What's the job? I haven't got heaps of qualifications.'

'We're running a 'get to know how to use a computer' course and the girl who was coming in to do it has just broken her leg. Then I saw you sitting there this morning and I know how skilled you are at helping people use these computers,' said Anne.

'I'm really not sure I could do it.'

'Of course you can. Mostly it's older people who want to know how to use e-mail or search the internet. You might get one or two who want to learn the basics of Word. Are you up for it? The course starts tomorrow.'

Kvanita, took a deep breath. It might only be for six weeks but it should give her a reference. 'Yes,' she replied.

Her mind was buzzing with ideas. Two hours later, after looking through all the plans and lists of people coming to attend the course. She picked up her bag to leave.

'Oh can you complete this application form and bring it in tomorrow? And I'll need your bank details. If you haven't an account yet either open one tomorrow or give us your Gran's details.' Anne said as she was leaving.

Kvanita took the form smiling and placed it carefully in her bag, knowing that she wouldn't be able to fill in all the details. She had no qualifications and no address. The librarians thought she was home schooled by her Gran so perhaps the lack of qualifications wouldn't be a problem, but no address certainly was.

Her mood plummeted but outside the sun was shining. She dawdled along the road on her way back to the garden shed. While she was grateful to have a roof over her head the evening stretched out before her. When she reached the other side of town she passed a road called Warwick Avenue. That name seems familiar, she thought and then she remembered why. It was where her father lived. Perhaps he's still there. Without thinking she turned to walk up the road. She'd just take a look at the house. No-one from round here would recognise her now. She was tall and very thin. Her hair was lighter than it used to be and there was no fear in her eyes. She walked on the opposite side of the road to where she used to live.

As she approached her old house loads of memories flooded back; both happy and sad, like her mother singing her a bedtime song. Then she remembered cooking cakes with her mum for dad's birthday. They had been a loving family once. Then dark memories came; an empty house where she was left on her own. Her father screaming at her and hitting her because, she realized now, he was grieving. How frightened she'd been.

The house stood in front of her now. The garden was filled with those large daisies she'd loved as a child. She was surprised how well kept the garden was. Obviously her father had moved on. Last time she'd seen the garden, it had been full of rubbish, including lots of beer bottles and cans. The door opened and an old man came out with his gardening gloves and a trowel. She looked at him again. He was slow like an old man but she realized he was not that old as he looked straight at her.

'Kvanita? Is it you?' She turned to run. 'No please stop and talk to me. I love you and I'm so sorry how I treated you. Is it you Kvanita?'

'I'm not coming in,' she said.

'We could talk here. I don't care. I'm the happiest man alive. I thought you were dead. I thought I'd never see you again.'

'I didn't know you cared,' she said in a voice that shocked her by its anger.

'I loved your mum and when she died I thought I'd died too. I should have cherished you and looked after you but all I could think about was how it wasn't fair that she'd died. Drink was the only thing that dulled the pain but it made me such an awful person. I don't drink at all now.'

'Good for you,' she said.

He sighed. 'I'm so sorry. You're right not to forgive me. I will never forgive myself. Won't you come in and tell me about your life? I could make us tea. Please.'

'There's nothing of interest to tell.'

'Where are you living? Who's been looking after you?'

Kvanita thought of the Gran. She wiped a tear away with the back of her hand. Suddenly her father was there with his arms round her. She wanted to push him away but she also wanted him to keep her safe.

'Let me make you some tea. You don't have to tell me anything. Let's just spend some time together. Perhaps we can learn to be a family again.'

He went inside the house and left the door open. She followed him in. She knew several ways to take care of herself if he turned nasty but she could see he was not the same angry man she remembered.

He handed her a scalding mug of tea and placed a big slice of coffee cake in front of her. Then he kept talking, but asked her questions so that she could join in if she wanted. Suddenly she found she'd told him about the Gran and how she'd died.

'You must come back and live here. Your room's still here. I'd love you to come home.'

'No Dad. I'm not being cruel but I don't know you. I don't know whether I can forgive you. Let's just take things slowly and see how they go.'

He looked so disappointed that she almost agreed to move in, but he might still be violent. She wasn't going to risk it.

'I just want to help you. I don't want to lose touch,' he said.

'You can help me. You can let me use this address for a few weeks. I want to open a bank account, and I will come and visit you so we can get to know each other again.'

As she left the house to return to her garden shed for the night, she felt happy. She had a job, she had an address, so she could complete her application form and maybe she had her father back. Tomorrow was the start of a new life and her first job. She would take the beautiful ancient vase to the police station; it could stay intact and then she would go to her father's house. Perhaps they could start again.

Just a Little Kindness

Vera, a little unsteady on her feet, tripped and fell down the hall steps, where the book club was held. Mrs Thumb soothed Vera.

'Come and sit down dear. That must've been such a shock for you.'

'Well I do feel a bit shaky.'

'Let me get you a nice cuppa tea.'

'Oh, thank you. You're such a warm person. I'm so lucky to have you as a friend.'

Mrs Thumb left the room and went to the kitchen. She switched the kettle on and took out a cracked mug from the cupboard.

Silly old bat, she thought to herself. *Can't even lift one foot up and put it in front of another.*

She poured the nearly boiled water onto the teabag, pinned a smile back on her face and went back to deal with Vera.

The old lady took the cup with a shaky hand. Her splodgy mouth slurped up the tea. Mrs Thumb turned her head away at this unpleasant vision.

'Aren't you having a cup too?' Vera asked.

'No, dear, I've got to lock up the hall soon as I've got an appointment. Don't rush yourself though. Can I call someone to come and pick you up?'

'You're not ill, are you, dear?' said Vera.

'No, it's just a routine check up.'

'Well Mrs. Thumb, if you're seeing the doctor anyway I'd get him to look at that mole on your face. It's got a ragged edge and it's very dark. Have you had it long?'

Mrs Thumb took a deep breath. *How rude o the old cow, to mention the mole on her face!*

'Thank you for your concern, Vera, but please don't worry about me.'

'But I can't help it, Mrs Thumb. I think it's got bigger lately. Don't you?'

'I'm sorry, but I do need to get going. Can I give you a lift Vera?'

Vera handed the cup back to Mrs. Thumb and hauled herself up. Her face was still pale and sallow. It was an unattractive face, tired and flabby.

'No, you're busy. I'm feeling much better now. I'll be off. See you next week.'

As soon as she'd gone, Mrs Thumb rinsed the cup and locked up. She made her way to her appointment. She could hardly have told Vera she was in a rush for a hairdressing appointment. Unconsciously her hand brushed the mole on her face.

What does Vera know about moles? she thought, as she hurried along the High Street. In fact she really shouldn't have mentioned it.

It was almost a year later that Vera died. Mrs Thumb, along with other members of the book club, attended Vera's funeral. She felt she had to go otherwise the rest of their friends would know how irritating she'd found Vera. As she sat there bored in the cold, unwelcoming church, she heard Vera being praised for the unselfish life she'd led, helping others as a cancer nurse. All her senses became alert. A cancer nurse! So she would have known about moles. Why, oh why hadn't she listened to her? Of course she knew the answer. She'd dismissed her as stupid, just because she was old. Tomorrow she would go to the doctor. She just hoped she wasn't too late.

Three Fat Ladies

Three fat ladies sat on the beach wall at Eastbourne. Their cherub faces defying the truth of age. They made an image like a comic picture postcard. Anne was the largest, weighing fifteen stone. She'd walked along the promenade to The Wish Tower, eaten her very large dinner, followed by a chocolate and banana sundae and now she was catching her breath, before making her way back to the hotel.

Linda had been slightly more restrained at lunch but she was still nearer thirteen stone than twelve.

Their mother, Ethel was well into her eighties.

'I don't know. You two are so unfit. I didn't need to sit down. I could've gone on walking,' she said, resting her hands on the bulge of her stomach.

'When I was your age I was never as large as you two. In fact, even now, you're both bigger than me,' said Ethel.

'Mother that's not a very nice thing to say,' said Anne.

'There's nothing wrong with telling the truth,' said Ethel.

'The fact is I do all the right things naturally. I've never wanted to drink. I've always eaten healthily and I walk every day.'

'Mother, wonderful as you undoubtedly are, you are not exactly tiny,' said Linda.

'Well maybe not, but I've never been as fat as you,' Ethel said with a sly little smile.

Linda turned to Anne and said, 'Do you fancy going on a diet, sis?'

'Yes, let's do it,' said Anne.

'What are you two saying?' demanded Ethel. 'It's rude to whisper.'

'We weren't whispering, Mother. If you'd wear your hearing aid you'd hear us.'

'I don't need a hearing aid.'

***

At the end of their week's holiday all three went their separate ways. Ethel went off to Australia for six months to visit David, her son. Linda returned to her job in the city and Anne to her husband.

During their time apart Linda started her diet. She also joined the gym. Far from being the trial she'd thought it would be, she found she enjoyed it. The gym gave her time to think while she was exercising. She began to find solutions to problems at work, while she was pounding the treadmill. She also started chatting to some of the people at the gym. But what she enjoyed the most were the fit young men. They were just so good to look at and as the weight fell off she noticed that some were looking back at her. Dan at forty, five years her junior, started inviting her out to play tennis or go for a walk. As Linda became more and more active, Dan became more and more interested. *Well I never*, thought Linda, *becoming slimmer is having all sorts of benefits.*

She phoned Anne to see how her sister was getting on with her diet.

'Well, you'll never believe this, but Rob's joined me on my diet and we're going for an hour's walk, after work, every day. I won't tell you what the side effects are, but let's just say Rob's a new man,' she laughed.

'And have you heard how mother's getting on with David?' asked Linda.

'Oh yes, David e-mailed me this morning. Apparently she's criticized his new wife one too many times. He's thinking about moving mother out to a hotel.'

'Why on earth would she do that?' said Linda.

'You know mother! It's her little vice, upsetting people, but perhaps being rude to a newly married daughter-in-law's not very clever. Oh well we'll see how she goes on.'

'Anyway shall we all meet up in Eastbourne again when she gets back in May?'

'Yes, I'll book the hotel.'

May came and the three ladies walked slowly to the Wish Tower for their lunch.

'So how are my two fat daughters?' said Ethel with a naughty twinkle in her eye.

Anne winked at Linda. 'We're fine mother and how was your trip to David's?'

'Oh it was alright I suppose, but they've a very small place. I had to move out to a hotel in the end. David came to see me every day but SHE wouldn't come.'

'You hadn't upset her had you?' said Anne.

'Of course, not. What on earth would make you think that?'

They arrived at their table and took off their coats. Ethel looked at each of them in turn and pressed her lips together.

Surely she would comment on how good they looked, thought Linda, but Ethel remained silent.

'Why Linda, you're looking well and so smart in that outfit,' said Anne.

'Well, you don't look so bad yourself, Anne. In fact you're looking remarkably slim,' smiled Linda.

Ethel scowled. 'I suppose you're both going to tell me now that I'm the fattest.'

'We wouldn't dream of it,' said Linda.

'Indeed not,' said Anne, 'that would be just too unkind.'

Forest Gems

Paul pressed the button on his entrance intercom.

'Yes, who is it?'

'It's Micky and John from uni. We were just passing and thought we'd pop in.'

'Just give me a minute,' said Paul. 'Now what do they want?' He hadn't seen them for three years. Still he supposed he'd better let them in.

He pressed the buzzer again and the door clicked open.

'Hiya, do come and sit down. It's been a long time. What have you two been up to?'

They both stank of smoke and stale sweat, but Paul smiled towards them.

Forget us,' said John. 'We saw you in the Mail. Fancy you finding the biggest truffle at 1.5 kg. That must have been huge. Great that you made so much money on it.'

'Well, John, first it was my dog that found the truffle and second the money went to the hospital that looks after me, so if you're after a loan...'

'Don't be daft,' said John, 'we don't want your money but why don't we all go for a walk in the forest. You never know we might just find another.'

Paul smiled. *People don't change*, he thought.

'OK, just let me get myself sorted.' He'd leave the back door open. It was always safe round here. He slipped on a light jacket and felt in the pocket for the small cold whistle and his keys. Then he reached up to the peg and took down the lead. Trixie ran to him and he could hear her snuffle of excitement as she sat while he attached it to her collar.

'Let's go then. You lead out.' Paul could hear John and Micky scuffle out of the room ahead of him.

'Shall we take the car?' asked Micky.

'It's two minutes up this lane. You can see the forest from here,' said Paul.

'I thought you couldn't see,' said Micky, 'have you recovered?'

Paul took on a long slow breath, 'No, but I can smell the forest and I walk there every day.'

'Ahh,' said Micky taking Paul's arm. 'We don't want you falling over, do we?'

Paul stopped himself saying he was blind, not drunk. 'Know much about truffles do you?'

'No, nothing, but Trixie will guide us. If she'll do it for you, she'll do it for us, won't she?' said John. 'So tell us, where do you sell your truffles?'

'Oh at the pub in the village; The Farmer's Arms.'

Paul could tell he was being led over to the bench at the edge of the forest.

'Take a seat, Paul and enjoy the sunshine. We'll just borrow Trixie for half an hour and pick you up on the way back,' said John firmly taking the lead from Paul.

'Hey hold on; just let me tell you how she works best. First you'll need to take her off the lead. You might as well leave it with me. Then you need to say, 'silvicola' and 'go girl'. Then just follow where she leads and dig up the fungi where she sits. Give her a pat and stroke and say it again and she'll go and find another. Got that?'

'Sillvicker?' said John.

'Sil –vic- o-la,' said Paul. Trixie came up and snuffled into his hand. He gave her a pat and took off her lead. 'Good girl Trixie. Silvicola, go girl,' he said. 'Micky, John, you'd better catch up I can hear she's off.'

'Won't be long,' called Micky over his shoulder as two sets of thudding footfalls set off after the light patter of his dog's feet.

He allowed himself a minute to breathe in the fresh air, as the gentle sun brushed his face with warmth. He could hear birds squawking alarm calls as the trio crashed through the forest. The scent of pine trees behind him was strongest. He imagined the big broadleaved and pine trees they were passing under and the little saplings struggling for light. Twigs cracked and rustling sounds reached his ears. Why did people think that because he was blind he couldn't keep up with them? It was so frustrating that people were basically so thick, especially people who'd spent years with him. Then he remembered that John had only achieved an ordinary degree and Micky had failed. Perhaps he shouldn't be so unkind. Occasionally he heard Trixie bark which meant she'd found another one for them. He smiled. Their sounds were getting distant. He couldn't risk her being out of earshot, so he felt in his pocket for the little whistle, took it out and blew it.

Trixie was his new dog and being trained at the moment, but he knew she understood the meaning of the urgent call he'd sent, even though he couldn't hear it himself. Soon the regular pattern of pattering became louder.

'Good girl,' he said as he slipped on her lead. He jogged back to the cottage holding the taut lead firmly.

Half an hour later a car started in the lane. He'd wondered if - almost hoped - they might have called in on their way back to show him their booty, but John was always greedy. He wouldn't want to share.

Within an hour the phone rang. 'Very funny!' said John.

'This isn't the right time to look for truffles, but would you have believed me if I'd told you that? That Mail article was just a filler for them and it was put in by someone who didn't know their fungi. Anyway how much did Gary from The Farmer's Arms give you for the silvicola?

'He laughed 'til tears ran down his face. Then he gave us a fiver for our trouble. Said they were one of the commonest wood mushrooms.'

'Never mind John, you've had a nice day in the forest.' The phone at the other end of the line crashed down.

Time for a short walk before bedtime, he thought.

He locked the back door as this time he'd take both dogs with him. He put a lead on Trixie. Truffles, his old and trusted friend would walk beside him up the lane and didn't need a lead. Hopefully in a couple of weeks Truffles could train Trixie to find the valuable fungi. He'd been training her on finding Agaricus silvicola for the past few days and she'd picked it up quickly.

He thought back over the day with a wry smile. His old friends had always underestimated him.

Consequences

Karl couldn't believe he was stuck behind a lorry doing forty miles an hour. He was on a promise tonight as long as he stayed sober and was in before midnight. Tracy had been very clear; no more than one drink and he'd kept to his side of the bargain. Well, he'd had a beer straight after work, but that was so early in the evening it didn't count. Then he'd had a whisky before his meal. That'd been his drink. Wine with the meal didn't really matter as the food soaked it up and then he'd just had a small whisky after the meal and nursed it all evening, although perhaps it had been topped up once or twice.

Now it was 11:50 and he had ten minutes to do a fifteen minute journey, but that was possible. He put his foot down on the accelerator and pulled out to overtake the lorry. Suddenly he was blinded by bright lights. He shielded his eyes. Then there was blackness. Distantly he heard a loud thud. He could see in his rear view mirror that the lorry had pulled to a halt. He fleetingly thought about stopping but the moment passed. He wanted to get home.

***

Simon, in the other car, turned the wheel sharply, just before the oncoming car would've hit him. He shot across the road and stood on the brakes. The thud of his car hitting the fence was followed immediately by the thud of hitting the telegraph pole. The car stopped. He threw the door open, unclipped the seatbelt and almost fell out. The cold of the night hit him. His first thought was of his son. Would he make it to Tommy's fifth birthday party tomorrow?

'Hey mate, are you alright? C'mon we need to get you off the road before someone hits you.' The strong arms of the lorry driver guided him to the grass embankment and sat him on a log in a driveway. Simon heard the man phone for the police. Distantly he heard voices and saw the lorry driver talking to a woman who'd just come out of the nearby house. He started to feel cold and then he found he was shivering uncontrollably.

Vaguely he became aware of blue flashing lights. 'That must mean the police had arrived', he thought. Soon a thick blanket was put round his shoulders and someone handed him a hot water bottle in a furry tiger cover. He realized he was holding it as if his life depended on it. He looked over to his car. It had been crushed like an old tin can. How would he get to Crewe tonight?

'I'll have a word with you in a minute sir, as soon as I've spoken with this witness,' said the policeman turning to the lorry driver.

'Now what's your name and can I have the details about what happened here tonight?'

'Derek Brown, officer. I was on my way to Chester, doing 40 miles an hour – y' know – keeping to the speed limit, when I noticed this total idiot driving far too close. It was a blue BMW. Anyway I couldn't believe it when he pulled out to overtake. There was clearly something coming the other way. This man here,' he said looking at Simon. 'Poor sod, didn't stand a chance. If he hadn't reacted so quickly he would've been dead.'

'Thank you Mr Brown. Please could you just write down your contact details and then you're free to go on your way.'

Mrs Carter came out from the house again. 'Can I offer anyone a cup of tea?' she asked.

'I'm just giving this man a few more minutes to see if he'll recover from the shock. I don't want him to have a drink in case he needs to go to hospital, but thanks anyway.' He then took out a phone and called a number. 'Hello, is that Scottish Power's emergency number? – P.C. Butler here. A telegraph pole's been hit; number 72 on the A51. I'm afraid there's a mains electricity cable hanging down across the road. It's well clear of cars but my colleague's having to stop any lorries and measure that they'll clear it. Can you send someone straight away?'

Simon began to feel warmer. He was lucky. Yes he was alive and tomorrow he'd be with his son. Shame about the car but hey, it could've been worse. He stood up and stretched his muscles.

P.C. Butler took all of Simon's details, after the breath test, and called him a cab. 'I'll get your vehicle moved but it looks beyond repair to me. Let me give you an incident number for your insurance company and here's a card with my number if you need any further information.

Simon sat in the back of the cab, feeling happy. Perhaps he was having a rush of adrenaline. He wished he'd been a better husband and paid more attention to his wife. He wished he hadn't spent so much time at work that she'd gone off with the gorgeous Gary, but he had a son who loved him and his wife encouraged him to visit. He'd have a lot to sort out tomorrow; getting a new motor, insurance claims, but he was ALIVE.

Karl put his key in the door at 12.01, but Tracy was smiling, so all was alright with the world. He couldn't really work out why those bright lights had disappeared. One minute they were there and the next they'd gone and why had the lorry stopped? Very strange, but at least he was home in time.

'Had a good evening?' Tracy asked.

'Yes, very quiet, but nice meal,' he leaned forward to kiss her and almost overbalanced.

'Urggghh, you've been drinking again,' she said darting out of his reach and flouncing off upstairs. 'Sofa for you tonight,' she called over her shoulder.

Karl punched a cushion. After all that! She really was a cold bitch.

He slept late the next morning, still in his work suit. He slept through the vacuuming and Tracy banging about in the kitchen. Karl even slept through the doorbell.

Finally he woke to Tracy's voice, 'He's in here P.C. Butler,'

His head throbbed. Karl didn't catch most of what was said until he heard, 'Karl Scott, we're arresting you for dangerous driving last night and causing an accident. You'll have to come to the police station with us now for an alcohol test.'

Karl opened his mouth to protest but before he could P.C. Butler said, 'Would you like me to ask your wife what state you were in when you arrived home?'

Karl looked to Tracy for support, but she shook her head in disgust and walked away.

The Night Visitor

Ethel sat bolt upright in the hotel bed. It was not that it was an uncomfortable bed; far from it. Something had woken her. As her eyes became used to the darkness she realized that she could see an old lady sitting at the end of her bed. Light was seeping in from the corridor, under the door and reflecting on a little woman in a pale nightgown.

'Oh you gave me such a fright,' said Ethel. 'What are you doing in my room and how did you get in? I locked the door.'

'I don't remember how I came to be here, but I'm sure this is my room, although if I'm honest my mind has been a bit fuzzy lately.'

'Well now, my mind isn't fuzzy and I booked into the hotel today and was given this room. What number were you given?'

'It was 221.'

'Now that is strange because this is 221,' Ethel said leaning over to switch on the bedside lamp.

The old lady's complexion was very sallow and she didn't look too well. Her pale green eyes were rather watery and her wispy hair uncombed. Ethel decided to take charge of the situation. She couldn't go and wake the whole hotel up in the middle of the night, so she eased her legs out of bed and tucked her feet into velvet slippers. Then she pulled her bed jacket round her shoulders and went over to the wardrobe.

'Let's see if we can make you comfortable and we'll sort your room out in the morning. I'm sure I saw spare blankets and pillows in the wardrobe.'

Ethel pulled out the comfy chair and put the dressing table stool next to it, to make a bed. Then she propped up the pillow and lifted the lady into the chair. She was as light as a feather. Tucked up in the woollen blanket the old lady looked even smaller.

'Is that a little warmer? Now what's your name?' asked Ethel.

'You're being so kind. Thank you. My name is Mavis.'

'Why don't you tell me what you can remember?'

'Well I booked in today, Friday and I remember having dinner in the dining room. The waiter was rather dishy and he smiled at me. Then I came up here and watched some television and went to bed. The next thing I know I'm sitting at the end of your bed, but I don't remember getting out.'

'Hmmm,' said Ethel, 'there's no clue there then, except you seem to have lost Saturday. I booked in on Saturday. I don't suppose you left on Saturday and went somewhere and have forgotten. Perhaps a relative? '

'No,' said Mavis. 'I came down to see my daughter. I went round to her flat just before I came to the hotel, but she wouldn't see me. We had a row, must be ten years ago now, and she's never forgiven me.'

'Perhaps we should go there tomorrow, just to check. Maybe she changed her mind.'

'No she won't have. I wanted to make it up with her before it's too late, but she didn't want to know.'

'Goodness me, what was the row about?'

'Oh I really don't remember; something and nothing.'

Although Ethel was tired she could never resist a bit of gossip and this did sound interesting.

'You can tell me. You'll never see me again after tomorrow and I'm the last person in the world to judge anyone.'

'It all started when she was living with that husband of hers in one of those big houses on Thornton Parade. I was getting tired and I couldn't be bothered doing all the cooking and cleaning in my little place and they had so many spare rooms, so I went round to stay and moved in.'

'Oh I don't think my daughter would like it if I did that,' said Ethel. 'She'd have me to live with her but she'd want to prepare and get things organized first.'

'I didn't give her that chance. She'd have said no if I had and she wasn't pleased. He didn't like it either. He was furious. Anyway I'm ashamed to say I got a bit jealous; I mean I'd never lived anywhere so lovely and the two of them were so in love. It wasn't fair.'

'So what happened?' said Ethel.

'I just pointed out his faults and then I started to help to create them.'

'What d'you mean?'

'I kept putting his coat on the floor and moving his shoes to the middle of the room; dirtying their bath. You know, that sort of thing. I know I shouldn't have tried to stir trouble between the two of them but I was very lonely.'

Ethel looked at the tiny woman sitting nested in the blanket. She could only feel pity, although she couldn't imagine anyone being jealous of their daughter. You'd just be pleased they were happy.

'Anyway,' continued Mavis, 'she caught me squeezing his toothpaste out over their sink and realized what I'd been up to. She made me go back to my rented rooms, but they split up very soon after that. Now she lives on her own in those flats in Weybourne Street.'

'Well that's an odd thing. My sister lives there. I'm visiting her tomorrow. How sad your daughter and her husband split up. Did she blame you?'

'Yes, never forgave me, but I couldn't have split them up unless they'd had problems, could I?'

'Oh don't ask me. Now are you comfortable? D'you think we should get some sleep?' said Ethel.

'I suppose so. It must be very late,' said Mavis.

The rest of the night passed quietly. Ethel woke up with the sound of her alarm and went across to where Mavis was sleeping. Mavis wasn't there. The blanket was still arranged in a little nest. She went to look in the bathroom but it was empty so she thought she'd check the corridor but found that the door was locked. Ethel packed away the spare blanket and pillow, dressed herself and went down to reception. The lady behind the counter looked at her strangely and said that no lady called Mavis had come to talk to her. It was a mystery thought Ethel, but there was nothing more she could do.

At breakfast she sat looking out of the window and thought about her own problems. Since Ken had died, she'd been lonely. Her daughter had invited her to live with them and she loved them all so much, but perhaps she would get jealous like Mavis had. How ridiculous; she would only ever wish her daughter to be happy, but still did she want to go and live there? The waiter came and gave her a broad smile and asked if she'd like more tea. He *was* very good looking.

After breakfast she made her way over to her sister Gwen's flat in Weybourne Street and was greeted warmly.

'You'll never guess,' said Gwen, 'you know the lady that died at the hotel you're staying at, well she's the mother of my neighbour. Nasty piece of work, according to her,' Gwen said nodding towards her neighbour's flat. 'Still there's always two sides to every story. Oh I hope you weren't given her room.'

'Actually I think I was,' said Ethel, 'although I didn't know someone had died until you just mentioned it.'

Strangers in our midst

Jodie looked down at the telephone number. Her heart was racing. Should she pick up the phone now? She took a deep breath and tapped out the number. It seemed ages before a woman answered and then the line crackled.

'Hello, my name is Jodie Long. I understand that you've agreed to speak to me. Is now a good time to talk?'

'Hello Jodie. Yes now's fine. I suppose I knew you might come and try to find me at some point and that's why I've agreed to speak to you.'

'I just wondered if we could meet up to have a chat?' said Jodie.

'To be brutally honest,' Margaret answered. 'I don't want to meet up. I don't wish you any harm obviously, but I gave you away. Since then I've had a child that I've brought up. I'm sorry but I've got to think about him. I love him so much. It would be such a shock to him to find out he's not my only child.'

'Couldn't we just meet once? He's had you all his life. All I'm asking is an hour over coffee.'

'Jodie, it would start a relationship with you that I don't want to have. I don't want to hurt those I love. I don't want to hurt my husband and son. I'm really sorry.'

'Why did you agree to speak to me then?' said Jodie.

'Because I felt I owed you a conversation on the phone. Have you got loving parents?'

'My parents had a child of their own in just under a year after they had me. They treated me well, but guess who they loved the most?'

There was a pause. Was her mother struggling with her self-pity? She'd been determined not to play the guilt card, but how else could she get her mother to want to see her?

'I'm sorry if your life hasn't been what you would have wished for but you're an adult now. You can make your own life; be anything you want. It's up to you now. Anyway I think it will be better for us both if you don't call again. Good-bye Jodie.'

'It'll be easier for you,' said Jodie and she held the phone to her ear long after the line went dead. At least she hadn't cried.

The next day Jodie went out to look for a job. She was staying in a bed and breakfast but her money was running out. She had some good qualifications but she wanted to stay in the area where her mother lived to find out more about her. She spotted the notice, 'Staff Wanted' in a cafe where a number of young people had gathered. As she went in the cafe owner was rushing around. He welcomed her enquiry and asked if she could start now. Jodie quickly picked up what needed to be done, which allowed the owner to go back to what he liked to do; the cooking.

Jodie actually found herself enjoying going to work. She was always busy and there was lots of chat from the young people who frequented the cafe. Sometimes when an older lady came in she fantasized that it was her mother, but how would she ever know? Soon she became part of a large group who included her in their activities. In amongst this group were Tony and Nick. They were a few years younger than her and obviously in love. Jodie liked them both. One evening Nick said to her that Tony had something to ask her.

'Mother is always trying to get me to bring my girlfriend home. I haven't told her about Nick. I just wondered if you'd come back with me. Pretend to be my girlfriend. I'm off to university at the end of the Summer, so that should keep her happy until then.'

'Sorry Tony. I'm really not sure about deceiving your mum. If you told her about Nick she might surprise you and understand that girls aren't on the agenda.'

'You've gotta be kidding. Margaret Pierce is as homophobic as they come. Tony is her perfect boy. She's booked him to get a first at Cambridge and to produce 2.4 children by the time he's thirty,' said Nick.

Jodie took a deep breath; Margaret Pierce. So she was sitting here with Tony her half brother. She smiled at them both.

'Are you sure it's a good idea? At some time you'll have to tell her,' said Jodie.

'When I've finished university I'll tell her. Well actually I'll tell dad first, but at some point she'll have to know. I'd like to be a bit older when I break the news,' said Tony.

Jodie took a deep breath. This was her chance to see her mother. Right or wrong, she had to take it.

'Ok, I'll do it but I'd like to be known as Jo Warner. If I'm going to be dishonest, I'd rather not use my own name.'

Both Tony and Nick kissed her on the cheek and they arranged for Tony to pick up Jodie on Sunday. Jodie felt badly about not telling Tony that she was his sister, but by doing so she would betray her mother's secret. In spite of the cold reception she'd received she couldn't bring herself to cause trouble.

Sunday came and Jodie dressed with care. She put on a purple patterned dress and low heels. Her brown hair was brushed until it shone and she carefully applied light make up.

'You look beautiful,' said Tony. 'Thanks for doing this.'

'I really like you and Nick and I'm not at all sure this is the best thing for you to do but if we're going ahead, let's go.'

Tony pulled up in front of a large detached house, with a neat garden. The front door opened before they'd reached it and there stood her mother. She formally shook Jodie's hand and welcomed her to their home. Mr Pierce gave her a bear hug and he gave Tony a nod of approval. The house was immaculate and the conversation polite. Margaret asked Jodie lots of questions.

'You seem to be older than my son,' said Margaret.

'Mother leave Jodie alone,' said Tony.

Margaret looked more carefully at Jodie and then asked her to come and help her bring in the second course. As soon as they reached the kitchen, Margaret shut the door.

'What are you playing at Jodie? You can't date your own brother. I can't believe that you're stringing him along. How dare you?'

'Tony and I are just friends. You have nothing to worry about.'

At that moment Tony burst in through the door.

'Do you need some help mother?'

'Oh Tony, you're such a lovely lad. I'm sorry but Jodie has just told me that she's moving away. She's been worrying about how to tell you.' Margaret gave Jodie a warning look. 'She knows you'll be disappointed but you'll be busy at university. Now's not quite the right time to have a girlfriend.'

'Oh mother, you're hopeless. I was here the day Jodie phoned. I had a hangover and was still in bed. You didn't realize I was even in the house. I must've reached the phone seconds after you. I probably wouldn't have done anything about it but then this girl called Jodie started working in the cafe we all go to and I liked her. In fact we all like her.'

Margaret's mouth opened as if to speak and then closed again. Jodie went over to Tony and gave him a hug.

'I'm so glad you know Tony. I only realized who you were this week, but I couldn't say anything because it was your mother's secret,' said Jodie.

'Welcome to the family,' said Tony.

'Well you've both given me such a fright. I thought for a moment that you were dating your own sister. I just knew you'd be trouble,' Margaret said turning towards Jodie.

'Well as this is a day for revealing truths, you'd better know that I'm dating Nick,' said Tony. 'We're not just friends.'

Margaret staggered back towards a kitchen chair and sat down.

Mr Pierce had stood quietly in the doorway listening to all the revelations. He went over to his wife and put an arm around her.

'It'll all be fine dear,' he said. 'We've all got a lot to get used to but there's the rest of the summer ahead of us. Welcome to the family Jodie and next weekend Tony, you can bring Nick round for Sunday lunch.' Then he turned to Margaret, 'It's time you got to know both your children.'

If Only

Marjorie was wearing shorts and trainers, ready to go for her run as soon as the drizzle stopped. She was looking out of the snug window when she saw a rabbit poke its head out of a burrow and quickly disappear again. How she wished she could disappear.

Her sister's baby was screaming again. Why couldn't Geraldine keep him quiet for five minutes? She was probably painting her nails or doing something equally puerile. If only it would stop raining she could get out and get some fresh air. The feeling of being trapped threatened to consume her. Her eyelids ached from being up all night looking after little Gerry. Geraldine had been completely out of it, having downed two bottles of Merlot. She felt so sorry for little Gerry but if she kept stepping in, then Geraldine was never going to take back the reigns of motherhood.

The screaming continued. It was just at that pitch that made Marjorie want join in. She needed to do something. Quickly she ran upstairs and checked that little Gerry was safe in the playpen; then she went to see that her sister was conscious. Finding Geraldine lying on the sofa with her earphones on, listening to loud music, Marjorie whipped them out.

'I need these for my run. I'll be about two hours. Little Gerry needs some milk and a cuddle, so you need to get off your backside. See you.'

Marjorie saw her sister's shocked face but gave her no time to respond. She sprinted downstairs, grabbing her bag and car keys and banged the front door loudly.

The rain wasn't heavy, but it was relentless. It trickled down her face and the back of her neck. She took her usual route along the side of the canal, across the fields and back round on the road. All the way she was hoping little Gerry was being looked after. What if she'd got this wrong and Geraldine just couldn't take care of him? By the end of the run her trainers were ruined. She'd splashed through muddy puddles and across spongy grass. She hadn't enjoyed her run or sitting in a cafe afterwards; all the time worrying about her nephew but somehow she had to get her sister to take responsibility for little Gerry. As she opened the front door she wondered what she would find. There was silence! There was no crying and nobody was walking around. She checked the rooms downstairs and then crept upstairs.

There was no noise. She checked her sister's room and found all the drawers and cupboards open. Heart beating fast she ran to the nursery but the cot was empty. On the floor by the door lay little Gerry's blue rabbit. She picked it up and smelled his baby smell. How could she have been so stupid? She wanted her sister to start looking after her baby. She hadn't wanted either of them out of her life. All this time she thought she'd been supporting them, but now she realized how much they had brought into her empty life. She remembered all the times she'd been resentful of losing a night's sleep when she should have seen what a privilege it was to look after her nephew; to see his wonderful smile and kiss his hair. Marjorie wiped her damp cheek with the back of her hand.

The harsh ring of the phone broke into her thoughts and she rushed to pick it up.

'You'll never guess what happened when you went out,' said Geraldine, 'Mark called round. Said he was so sorry and missed us both. He's bought a house for us so we can be a proper family. He only gave me five minutes to pack as he said either I wanted to be with him or I didn't.'

'That's wonderful news, sis. I'm so pleased for you. Where's this new house?'

'It's in Liverpool. We're on our way there now. Thanks so much for letting us stay. I'll be in touch next week. Bye.'

Marjorie sat staring at the phone long after it had gone dead. She was glad she hadn't caused Geraldine to leave but the quiet in the house was deafening. And Liverpool was two hundred miles away.

Killer's Lost Bark

Killer looked at the bowl of heaped food in front of him. He couldn't believe Wayne was giving him such a treat. It was a shame that he'd tied him in the yard again, as not being able to wander where he wanted, took the edge off the joy of the big meal in front of him.

'Guard the house, Killer,' Wayne called as he went through the back gate and into the alley.

The words Wayne had said meant nothing to Killer, but he recognised his name and understood that Wayne was going out. He might as well eat the food. There was nothing else to do. When his belly was full he lapped up some water and settled down on the warm tarmac for a sleep. All seemed well with his world.

The next day dawned and Killer drank the rest of his water. There was no food in his bowl, but he often missed a day's food when Wayne forgot to feed him. The sun grew hotter. He decided to bark in the hope that Wayne had come back and would remember to feed him. He barked until his throat hurt and then Mrs Nosey Parker (that's what Wayne called her) poked her head over the fence and shouted at him. He understood that she was cross so he dropped down flat on the ground and she went away.

It was a long day. He panted to try to cool off but there was no shade until early evening. As the temperature dropped he started to pace the yard, back and forth. He was bored. He barked a little but Wayne didn't come out of the house. He tugged at the chain, until his neck became sore and then sank to the ground.

During the night he slept fitfully. Mrs Nosey Parker's cat came and sat on the wall and grinned at him in that unkind way, which said, 'you can't chase me'. Strangely he welcomed the company. He let her know he was hungry and thirsty but she just shrugged. There was nothing she could do about it.

Dawn came again. Killer was hopeful that this day would bring Wayne back. He was now very hungry and thirsty. He didn't get up or bark as it seemed to make the hunger worse. Mrs Nosey Parker looked over the fence, but unusually she didn't shout at him. The sun burned down onto him and his thirst was dreadful. Sleep came and went and he was aware that the cat came and sat quite close to him, but she wasn't tormenting him anymore.

The evening brought a down pour. Killer stayed where he was. There was no shelter he could reach. His coat became heavy and drips fell off his nose, his ears and lots of other parts of him. Then he started to feel cold and shiver. With his body shaking he finally gave in to feeling dejected and miserable.

'Where was Wayne?' He knew he annoyed Wayne from time to time, because he'd get a belt across his back or a kick to the legs, but he'd never been this thirsty or hungry.

In the morning he woke to silence. Then he heard the cat mew. She was sitting by his water bowl. He lifted his head, which felt unusually heavy. Someone had filled up his bowl. She ran off as he crawled over to it and drank and drank. 'How wonderful was water,' he thought. Feeling a little better he checked out the food bowl but it was still empty.

Although Killer felt less thirsty, he was still very hungry. Then Mrs Nosey Parker came in through the gate. He really couldn't be bothered to get up and greet her, but he lifted his head and made a little bark. It came out as a bit of a whimper, which surprised him. She stared at him for a minute and then shook her head. He couldn't help feeling so ill. He'd have given her a proper bark if he could've managed it. It didn't look like Wayne would be back today. Luckily he wasn't feeling bored any more. He was just tired, so he settled down for a nap.

Time passed but Killer didn't know how much time. He heard people talking on the other side of the fence and one of them was Mrs Nosey Parker. Then she opened the gate again. In she came with a woman in uniform. He tried really hard to lift his head and greet them but his head had become too heavy.

There was some more talking and then his chain was being unhooked from the pole. Suddenly the uniformed woman was lifting him in her arms.

'Come on Killer,' she said. Her voice was gentle and soothing. Mrs Nosey Parker gave him a stroke on the back. 'Well, that's a first,' he thought. He rested his heavy head on the woman's soft front, until she settled him into a cage in the back of a van. She smelt of roses.

The afternoon went by in a blur of people. Gentle hands probed and prodded him. His eyes and teeth were looked at and then a smelly sticky stuff was rubbed into the back of his neck. He managed a few greetings but for some reason his voice had gone quiet. He was wondering what had happened to his beautiful bark when suddenly a wonderful food smell wafted through the air. A bowl was put down in front of him, containing some sludgy looking, mud coloured stuff.

'Not my usual biscuits,' he thought, 'but food was food. It was smooth but not as liquid as water.' Although he felt tired he licked the bowl clean. Then he was stroked and patted. Soon he fell asleep on a soft rug. Fleetingly he wondered if Wayne was around but then he thought of the lovely tastes in his mouth.

Within a few days he was going out for walks on springy fresh grass. He could smell the tantalising odour of other dogs, but couldn't see any, although he could hear them. Killer met lots of new people and felt much better now that he could say hello to them properly. His bark was back. He wondered if anyone was going to shout at him or give him a kick but nobody did. He couldn't believe all the strokes he was given and the food was delicious. He licked his lips just thinking about it.

Lots of people came and looked at him, but one day a boy called Will peered into his kennel. Will reached through the gate to stroke him. He liked Will's scent so he gave him a big lick. Will came over to him and spent time hugging him and patting him. Killer couldn't believe that anyone was a lovely as Will and enjoyed chasing him and following him around the field.

Killer liked everything about Will. He liked his size and his voice; he liked his scent and he loved the cuddles. Before Will left he gave him another big lick and enjoyed listening to Will giggling.

Although he fell asleep happy he wished that he could spend more time with his new friend. Had anyone ever been so friendly to him? If they had, he couldn't remember it. Several days later Will turned up again and attached a lead on his collar. He wasn't sure what was happening as so many people patted him, but eventually he was sitting on the back seat of a car, next to Will.

Somehow Killer understood that he was going to spend a lot of time with Will in the future. Happiness washed over him. In the back of his mind he knew he'd lived somewhere else, with someone else, but the memory of Wayne had faded.

'It's amazing how good life can be,' he thought as Will tickled him behind the ear. He rested his head on Will's lap in perfect contentment.

A Hard Day's Night

Hilary stood outside the Odeon, wearing her Mary Quant style dress. It was a very short tent dress, black and gold check and made of light corduroy material. She shivered. There was no point in having a fashionable dress and covering it with a thick coat. Her stomach was churning over. Nick was due any minute. He was older than her by two years and if her dad had known she was meeting him, she would have been grounded for ten years. Nick was very tall, over six foot and he had the bluest eyes she had ever seen.

Her dad thought she was going to see 'A Hard Day's Night' for the third time. He was happy to accept her obsession with the Beatles, but couldn't cope with the idea that his little girl might be interested in boys of the real variety. If he'd known that she was not with her friend, Christine, tonight, he'd have forbidden her leaving the house. As it was, he'd not been happy with the length of her skirt, and she'd had to put her make-up on after he'd dropped her off.

Then she saw Nick as he turned the corner into the main high street. He waved at her but she noticed he didn't speed up. He was smart in a leather jacket and tight jeans that had been specially faded to give a casual look. He greeted her with a kiss on the cheek and suggested that they go to this party he knew about in a nearby hall. She felt the warmth of her hand in his and forgot how cold she'd been feeling. It was amazing how being in love had such an effect.

The hall looked beautiful to Hilary; it was bright and decorated. Music was blaring out and people were dancing the twist. She felt very awkward and gauche. She had thought she looked fashionable but this crowd was sophisticated, older and she knew nobody but Nick.

'I'll get you a drink,' Nick said.

'Just an orange juice,'

'Yeah right,' he said, leaving her on her own.

She felt panic rising. She shouldn't have come. There were none of her friends here and her dress, which she'd spent all her Saturday job money on, was decidedly frumpy.

'Fancy coming out the back, love,' a boy leaned over her.

'No thanks. I'm with Nick.'

The boy, who introduced himself as Gary, laughed, 'Oh well you'll be out the back soon enough then.'

'What d'you mean?'

'Oh c'mon love, you must know his reputation.'

'No, I don't. Anyway we've only just met.'

The boy laughed again. 'Huh, that won't make any difference.' He wandered off as Nick returned with the drinks.

'Who were you talking to? Nick asked, handing her a drink.

'Someone called Gary. He er wanted to dance, but I said I was with you.'

She took a sip. 'What's this? It's not orange juice.'

'They didn't have any, so I got you an orange drink instead. If you don't like it leave it.'

Now she'd annoyed him. 'No, I'm sure it'll be fine,' she said taking a sip.

'Wanna dance?' Nick said, leading her on to the floor. They did the twist and then a smooch dance.

'You read Lady Chatterley?' Nick asked.

'Not exactly. It's been round school and I've read excerpts, but I couldn't take it home. My dad would kill me if he found it. '

'You frightened of him then?'

'Well, I don't deliberately annoy him. He's quite strict and my mother's even more so.'

'I'm surprised they let you come out without meeting me then.'

'They don't actually know. I'm not allowed boyfriends.' said Hilary.

She finished her drink and Nick went off to get her another one. This time she felt fine about being on her own and was swaying to the music when he came back. He smiled at her and she took a big thirsty swig. They danced some more. The lights dimmed and she was aware that Nick was very close and his hands were all over her. She tried to keep standing, but felt unsteady on her feet and then without warning she had to push him away. With her hand over her mouth she ran to the ladies and threw up. There was no-one about to help her and then the door opened. She turned round and saw Nick was there.

'Yuck, now that's not very enticing. I don't fancy you in that state. You'd best get yourself home to daddy, love.'

Hilary couldn't reply as another wave of nausea hit her. She heard the door slam. Tears ran down her cheek and as she finally looked up the sight in the mirror was horrendous. Nick didn't want to be with her. She had to get back to the Odeon before her dad picked her up and she looked a total mess.

Quietly the door opened again and Gary stood there with a pint glass of water. 'I thought you might be needing this, as I saw Nick dancing with Pam and I can guess how much Vodka he put in your drink.'

'Vodka? No wonder I was so ill.'

'Look I know I tried it on earlier, but I don't get girls smashed and then take advantage. Just drink the water slowly. The best thing you can do now is wash your face, clean yourself up, put some make-up back on and then walk out of this party with your head held high.'

Hilary looked at him carefully and then back at her image in the mirror. He made sense. She washed her face and reapplied her make-up, in between sipping the water. Once she'd brushed her hair and backcombed it again she looked much better.

'My stomach feels rough,' she said.

'Have some toast when you get in,' Gary said. 'It's probably a good job you threw up. At least you won't be so drunk.'

Hilary glanced at her watch. 'I must hurry. My dad's picking me up from the Odeon in twenty minutes.'

'C'mon then. Head high and smile as if you're happy. Hold onto my arm,' said Gary

Hilary walked back out into the main hall. The music was too loud and as she looked closely she saw what a tatty place it was.

'Night Nick,' she called as she sauntered out of the door. She turned to Gary when they were outside. 'I'm going to run as I daren't be late.'

'OK, I'll run with you,' said Gary.

It was cold, but the fresh air made her feel better. They arrived before her dad. 'I'll stand over there until you get into your dad's car, just to make sure you're safe. By the way Psycho is coming back to this cinema next Saturday. D'you fancy going? '

'If I can bring my friend Christine,' Hilary said.

Gary smiled and started to walk away. 'It's a date,' he called.

'Thank you for helping me tonight,' she shouted back as her dad's car drew up at the curb.

The Grey Lady

The church clock struck, breaking the early morning silence. A body lay slumped across the stone steps; the face hidden by a newspaper. No-one was around to see the grey figure that glided past the church wall.

The mist was still rising from the damp ground when Marcus, the curate, went to open the church. He loved this time in the morning. Everything in the world seemed alive and fresh. The wonderful smell of the countryside, the trees and grass, came to him as he walked up the lane towards St. Bede's. The birds were singing, dew covered spider webs glistened in the blackberry threaded hawthorn hedge. Their intricate lace fascinated him and he idly wondered where the spiders hid as they never seemed to be near their webs.

The gate made a protesting creak as he pushed it open, reminding him that he should oil the hinges. It was then he noticed something on the steps. He tried to remind himself that people meant well when they left their old clothes to be distributed to those less fortunate. The sad fact was that most things left were so well worn that they couldn't be passed on. It usually meant he had to arrange to take them to the tip.

As he walked further up the path he could see the bundle was large and bulky. Then he was running towards it. He was having difficulty breathing. His heart was banging against his chest. He noticed the feet first, brown leather walking boots, one sticking out at an odd angle.

Taking a deep breath, he carefully lifted the corner of the newspaper to peek underneath. There was no doubt the man was dead. Startled glassy eyes stared up at the sky. Stepping back he took his mobile phone from his coat pocket.

Soon the place was bustling with police and green paper suits. Photographs were taken and the area cordoned off. Marcus tried to remember if he'd ever seen the man before. Nothing came to him and yet he had a strange sense that he knew this man. There was something familiar about him.

On another day he would have thought it funny that Canon Wanton had been caught out, still in bed, at nine in the morning. John Wanton made it clear he wasn't available in the mornings because he needed to deal with correspondence and e-mails. The whole village knew however, that since his wife had left, he stayed up drinking until the small hours. Even so, Marcus covered for him as best he could. It was nearly a year since Barbara had run off, and although he did what he could to help John, he realized he was a little resentful of the extra duties he had to perform.

Just after the police arrived, Canon John Wanton turned up, wearing yesterday's clothes and smelling of stale beer. Marcus felt a sudden urge to protect the church's reputation.

'Why don't you go back to the vicarage and finish your breakfast? I'll answer any questions here. Then you can offer the police some coffee when they want to talk to you,' he said.

'Good idea,' mumbled John. 'I'll get Mrs. Wood to come and help. There'll be a lot of folk needing refreshments.'

As he shuffled off along the path, Marcus could only hope that John would take a shower and freshen up. The quiet joy of the early morning had certainly been shattered.

It was later that evening, as the day's light was fading, that Marcus returned to the church to finally oil the gate. The place was deserted. He took out the little yellow can, from the Sainsbury's carrier bag, when an icy draft whisked past his neck. Turning he saw the figure of a grey lady retreating round the side of the church building. Without thinking he dropped the can and followed her. She was running but not fast. He guessed she was past her youth. His long strides soon caught up with her by the Yew tree and he was about to call out, 'Don't be afraid,' when the woman turned to face him. She seemed oblivious of Marcus as if she was seeing something he could not see. A look of horror spread across her face. Her eyes widened. Mouth opened. Arms raised in front of her face. Then she crumpled to the ground.

Marcus was horrified. It was Barbara Wanton and she had vanished, like the morning mist, before his eyes. He stood there completely still until he realized his body was actually shaking with cold.

'Now sir, do you mind telling me what you're doing here?' said Constable White, breaking into the silence. 'Ahh, Curate Lovell, are you alright? You're looking rather peaky, if I may say so.'

Marcus couldn't speak. His mouth just wouldn't work. He tried but words just wouldn't come out.

'Come with me sir,' said Constable White, putting an arm round his shoulders as he led him back up the path towards the vicarage. They walked in silence for which Marcus was grateful. Of course he could tell no-one he'd seen a ghost. They'd think him completely mad. He'd tell the truth as far as he was able, but what did it all mean? Had he just watched Barbara being killed?

Sitting in front of an open fire, with a scalding hot mug of coffee in his hands Marcus began to feel better. Canon Wanton was on the sofa opposite and Constable White was perched on the other end.

'Now sir, you really need to tell me what you were doing at the crime scene at this time of night?'

Marcus looked at the two men on the sofa. P.C. White with his hands wrapped round a mug of coffee and John clasping a silver tankard of beer.

'I just went to oil the gate. I knew the police would be there, so didn't think it'd be a problem.'

'I was there,' said P.C. White. 'Just had a call of nature, if you know what I mean.'

Marcus's eyes looked over P.C. White's shoulder to where a photograph of Barbara smiled at him from the wall. He continued, 'I was just about to pour out the oil when someone dressed in grey ran behind me and I gave chase. I lost them and afterwards I wondered why they were there. I guess I couldn't believe that I'd followed them.'

'And was it a man or a woman?' asked the Constable.

'Mmmm, looked like a woman' said Marcus.

'You must stay here tonight old chap,' said Canon Wanton. 'Nasty business all of this.'

'No, I'm going back to my place. I'm O.K. now and I'll sleep better in my own bed. Besides I'm sure I know the man who died. I want some time on my own to think.' He stood up, paused in front of Barbara's photograph looking puzzled; then left.

That night as he drank endless mugs of coffee, trying to make sense of the day, he thought of

Barbara. Strange he hadn't noticed that photograph before. It must've always been there. And then he remembered where he'd seen the dead man. He was Barbara's lover. Marcus phoned the police station immediately and left a message for the inspector.

The next day there was a loud banging on his door. Inspector McCarthy walked passed him, without waiting to be invited in, waving a letter in his hand.

'No way to say this nicely. Do sit down.' Marcus obeyed. 'I'm afraid your mate Canon Wanton took his own life last night. He wrote you a note. I took the liberty to open it,' he said and handed Marcus the letter in a plastic bag.

Dear Marcus,

I can't carry on, knowing what I've done. I killed Barbara, but it was an accident. She said she was leaving me and I got angry and chased her. I confess I hit her - just the once- and that was it; the love of my life gone. I buried her under the Yew tree, where she fell. Then he turned up. He said he just wanted to speak to her but I was afraid and I killed him. I knew it was wrong, but I couldn't stop myself. In time you'd have remembered who he was. Then I'd be the main suspect. I couldn't face going to jail. Either I had to kill you or end this sorry mess.

Please say a prayer for me. No-one else will.
John Wanton

'You'll have to come and identify the body Mr Lovell, but when you're ready. There's no rush,' said Inspector McCarthy.

Later, as the sun was going down, Marcus went to the churchyard. There was no sound; no birds singing, not even the rustling of leaves. He stood by the ancient Yew tree and prayed that Barbara's nightmare was over. He prayed for them all and he never saw the grey lady again.

A Christmas Star

Rosie smiled at her daughter as she entered the nursery. Star, came running towards her, with arms raised ready to be picked up. She lifted Star in the air, twirling her around so that Star giggled in the way only a two year old can.

They went to the town for half an hour to look at the sparkly Christmas lights, which Star thought were magical. On the way home they popped into the supermarket, so that Rosie could buy some end of the day bargains. Back at their tiny flat she cooked cauliflower cheese, while Star chattered away. Rosie loved this time of day.

By the time Star was finally in bed and asleep it was eight o'clock. Rosie went to her work bag and took out the accounts. Her boss often sorted her out extra work to do at home in the evening. Although she was tired and would have loved to have an early night, she appreciated that it was this extra money, above her normal wages that allowed her to be independent and look after her daughter. She worked on into the night until her eyes were having difficulty focusing. Finally she was done and fell into bed. She was asleep within minutes.

Mornings were rushed, but those few moments with Star recharged her batteries. They chatted all the way through breakfast and the walk to the nursery. It was when she was back at work that Rosie wondered what the future held. Her parents had rejected her when she told them she was pregnant. She remembered their anger and how they tried to force her to get rid of the baby. Steve, her baby's father, had made it very clear from the start of their relationship that it was not long term. He was off to university at the end of the summer. Perhaps she should have told him about Star. Now she was in a dead end job, albeit with an employer who tried to help her. She needed to do something to change her life.

She looked forward to the weekend because she had a treat planned for Star. She'd found a local hall in the centre of town where Father Christmas was coming to call and each child would receive a small present. She knew Star would be so excited.

Rosie dressed Star in her best dress and warmest coat and wrapped her in a thick blanket in her pushchair.

'What will he be like, Mummy?' Star asked.

'Well I think he'll have a red coat and a long white beard. He'll ask you if you've been a good girl this year.'

'Have I been a good girl?'

'You're always a good girl. Here we are. We'll park the pushchair here and then we'll see if Father Christmas has brought an elf with him.'

She lifted Star out of the pushchair and they walked up the steps into the hall. As they entered it was as if they were entering a magical world. Glittering stars and baubles hung from netting draped in curves from the ceiling. A huge Christmas tree stood in the corner of the room with lights that twinkled off and on. There was even a wishing well. Rosie took out two coins and gave one to Star.

'You need to throw your coin into the well and make a wish,' said Rosie.

Star threw her coin, 'I wish we could have a daddy.'

Rosie's heart flipped. Where had that come from she thought? She'd never realized that Star knew that other children had daddies, but of course she had seen men picking up their children from the nursery.

'Throw the coin, mummy. Throw the coin.'

Rosie threw the coin and closed her eyes. She made her wish.

'What did you wish for?' asked Star.

'Oh I can't tell you, Star because it's a secret.'

They went to join the queue to see Father Christmas. Rosie could feel the excitement of all the children and parents who were chatting to each other. It was a lovely friendly atmosphere apart from the child directly behind them who was screaming.

'I want to go in now. I don't want to wait. All these silly people! I want to go in now.'

'Nicola, you'll have to wait.'

'Why should I? I want to go in now.'

The tantrum continued and Nicola, who was much bigger than Star, knocked her over, accidently. Star started to cry.

Rosie picked her up in her arms and cuddled her, 'You're alright darling. The little girl didn't mean to hurt you. Mummy kiss it better.'

'Say you're sorry Nicola.'

'I'm not sorry, stupid blubbermouth.'

Then the Elf appeared. She was dressed in a shiny green costume and a red wig with a little green cap.

'Father Christmas won't think you've been a good girl, if you aren't sorry when you hurt someone. He only gives good children a present.'

'Don't you start blackmailing my child. It was an accident and we've been waiting for the present a long time,' said Nicola's mother.

'Is it just the present you've come for?' asked the Elf.

'Of course it is. I'm nine. You don't think I believe in some silly old man, do you?' said Nicola.

The Elf disappeared and was back within ten seconds.

'Here's your present Nicola. I hope you have a happy Christmas.'

Nicola ripped off the wrapping paper as she walked out of the hall.

'It's a stupid jigsaw,' she was heard saying as she went through the door.

The Elf turned to the rest of the queue. 'Father Christmas is working as hard as he can. I hope the rest of you don't mind waiting.'

'Well we're happy to wait,' said Rosie. 'There's so much to see and it's all so pretty.'

Soon it was their turn. The flap of the den was lifted and Star hid behind her mother. Rosie picked her up and waited for Father Christmas to speak but although he had his mouth open, no words were coming out.

'Father Christmas, are you alright?' asked Rosie.

'Oh yes. Sorry. And who have we here?'

Star buried her head in her mother's shoulder.

'Say hello, Star.'

'Have you been a good girl this year, Star?' asked Father Christmas.

'I'm always a good girl. Mummy says.'

'And how old are you?'

'Two.'

'Is your daddy outside?'

'Excuse me, why are you asking her that?' said Rosie.

'I wished for my daddy with the coin,' said Star.

'Sorry,' said Father Christmas 'Here's your present,' handing over a present to Star.

They turned to leave.

'Oh and a little card for mummy,' said Father Christmas, busily writing on a parcel label.

Rosie stuffed it in her pocket and went to enjoy the rest of the day. It was not until Star was in bed later that evening that she went to her coat and retrieved the card. It said:

It's Steve. I've missed you. Can we catch up? 07787654231.

No wonder he'd had his mouth open. He must've taken a holiday job during his break at University. This would be his third year. She looked at the card again. Should she call him? Rosie thought about it but not for long. Star had wished for a daddy and the more she thought about it she realized Star was entitled to know her daddy. She thought about Steve. He had a right to know he was a dad. It would be hard to share Star, but Rosie knew that children had to have lots of relationships. She dialled Steve's number and agreed he could pop round that evening. She scooted round the flat tidying up and then dived into the shower. She had just applied some make-up when the door bell rang.

She opened the bottle of wine he'd brought round and they sat down to talk.

'I tried to call you several times but the phone was put down. I thought I'd done something to annoy you,' said Steve.

'No, my parents don't have a daughter anymore.'

'That's ridiculous. Why on earth would they cut you out of their lives?'

At that moment the door to Star's bedroom opened. She tottered over to Rosie, still full of sleep. 'I heard you talking mummy. Is this my daddy?'

What should she say? She hadn't even discussed it with Steve, but then she heard him say.

'I'd like to be your daddy, Star. Do you think I'd do?'

Star looked from Steve to Rosie.

'He is your daddy. I was going to tell you tomorrow.'

Star climbed on Rosie's lap and looked at Steve. Then she gave him a big smile.

'We'll ask daddy if we can see him tomorrow because it's bedtime now.' She lifted Star into her arms and carried her back to bed.

When she came back into the room Steve said, 'Why didn't you tell me?'

'You said that we were only for the summer as you were off to university. I didn't want you if you didn't want us.'

'But I did want you. That's why I phoned and phoned. I'm nearly through university. I can help with Star. I want to be a proper dad for her.'

'Let's just take it one day at a time. We'll take Star out tomorrow and see where we go from there,' said Rosie; but in her heart she was thinking that both their wishes had been granted.

'One day at a time is fine with me, as long as we end up all together,' said Steve as he pulled Rosie into his arms.

Witch Hunt

I could smell food cooking close by. My stomach responded to the aroma. After days of just water and stale biscuits I longed for something tasty. Automatically I walked faster. As I turned the corner I saw an old man sitting by a fire roasting some meat; probably rabbit. He was big and bald and although his back was slightly bent he didn't look to be past his strength. Nervously I walked towards him wondering if he would be friendly. I certainly didn't want any trouble. He heard my footsteps and turned towards me.

'Don't suppose you've enough to share?' I called, stopping where I was. I didn't want to look as if I'd grab his food and run.

He looked me up and down and then smiled. 'There's plenty of food, if you're on your own. Come and join me.'

I dumped my bag by the fire and sat on my black cloak. Brushing my long dark hair away from my face I let the flames warm me. It was the most wonderful feeling. Soon the meal was ready. I cannot describe how delicious it was. I wiped the juices away from my chin, with my hand and picked up the mug of strong black tea. It was not to my taste but I didn't want to offend my host.

'So why is a pretty young thing like you wandering around here on your own at this time of night,' he asked.

'I am Topaz. I live in Bycross Mill in the valley beyond and I am travelling to see my grandmother. She lives in Wootten Stanley. Somehow I seem to have taken a wrong turn and I don't recognise the landscape. I don't suppose you have a map.'

He took out a small map made from a linen backed material and placed it on the ground before me. He pointed first to Bycross Mill and then to Wootten Stanley. Then he showed me where we were. Past Wootten Stanley

'You are miles out of your way. It would be dangerous to travel tonight. You'd better stay here by the fire until the morning.'

'So, why are you here?' I asked.

He looked at me closely. 'You're looking tired,' he said. 'Lay down by the fire and I'll tell you who I am.'

He looked a kind man and he'd just fed me and offered me a place to rest for the night, so I spread out my cloak and lay down. He didn't move. The fire lent its rosy glow and I felt safe.

'My name is Volt Hunter. I'm hunter by name and by profession. I hunt witches and deliver them to the authorities.'

Fear spread through me and chilled my bones. I sat up slowly and schooled my voice to be calm. 'So you believe in witches, do you? I don't. Are you telling me you've actually met a real witch?'

'Who knows?' he smiled. 'I get paid for delivering them to the authorities and that's the end of my job. Do you know there's a witch on the run from Wootten Stanley at the moment? Let me show you her poster.'

He leaned over and passed me the poster. There in front of me was a drawing of my likeness. I handed it back to him.

'Poor woman. She will die a most excruciating death. I'm glad you know I'm not a witch.'

'Now how do I know that Topaz?'

'Well, it's obvious. I approached you for food. A witch wouldn't need to do that. A witch, if such beings exist, would be able to catch their own food; light their own fire. That's what they do isn't it?'

He smiled. 'I think you're missing the point, dear girl. I just have to deliver someone who looks like the poster and I get paid. You'll do, whether or not you're a witch.'

'So what happens now? Do you tie me up and haul me back to the village in the middle of the night?'

'No, Topaz. You lie down again and you will sleep. Your tea was drugged. You can be comfortable tonight. Tomorrow when we're both rested I'll take you to the village. It can be as easy or as hard as you like.'

'Don't you care what they'll do to me? And what about my grandmother? How can you condemn me to a death by drowning or by fire?' Doesn't it prey on your conscience? Do you have no concept of good and evil?'

'Lie down NOW, Topaz. I have to eat just like the next man. I have never killed any woman, witch or otherwise. If you really want to know what I think I'll tell you.'

I lay back down on my cloak.

'Yes, I really want to know.'

'Obviously there's no such thing as witches. These poor creatures have just annoyed someone powerful, but that's their problem not mine. I don't commit the murder. It's not my responsibility. In your case I think it's a terrible waste to kill someone so beautiful and young, but that's mankind for you. Now go to sleep.'

He got out a rug and lay down on the other side of the fire. Soon his snores could be heard rattling into the night. I sat up slowly and then stood up, quietly lifting my cloak from the ground. I wrapped it round myself. How lucky I had poured the tea into the ground behind me. It had smelt foul. I looked over at Volt Hunter and silently swore he would never cause another woman to die a terrifying death.

In the morning a tiny mouse woke up on the rug by the dying fire. I was walking in the fresh sunshine, listening to the birds. I laughed at the thought of how many predators there are for mice. He would be hunted every day of his life, be it a short one or a long one.

Green Duck

Eve tucked the letter into her coat pocket, as she wheeled the pushchair out of the front door. Her daughter was wrapped up warmly, with a thick padded coat, gloves and hat. Her feet were tucked into a woollen blanket. Eve pulled her scarf across her face to keep out the bitter cold. She remembered the terrible row she'd had with her father about Ian, three years ago.

'He's no good. He's a chancer and if you keep seeing him he'll ruin your life. I order you to stay at home.'

'I hate you,' she'd replied, 'you always try to stop me having any fun. You'll only be happy if I'm stuck here forever with you.'

Eve smiled to herself now. How unfair she'd been. Her dad had always held open house for all her friends and she remembered this clearly now, but she had only been sixteen when she'd left.

This morning Eve and Tilly had spent the morning unwrapping the small presents that Eve had managed to collect from car boot fairs and charity shops. Tilly's favourites had been the two tiny fairies that Eve had found in an old tin at the local boot fair. She had worked hard to make Christmas special for Tilly and had managed to decorate her flat with some decorations that her work had been throwing away. It was amazing what you could do with a little imagination. Eve started to sing Christmas carols as they walked along the road to the park. She could see her breath mist in front of her. In her basket she had a flask of warm soup and some sandwiches. It was an odd Christmas lunch but luckily two year olds are easy to please and Tilly was always a happy child.

'Feed the ducks. Feed the ducks, mummy,' said Tilly.

'Yes, Tilly we're going to feed the ducks.'

'See the green duck,' Tilly said, kicking her blanket off her legs.

'I hope we'll see the green duck, but I can't promise he'll be there. We'll have to wait and see.'

When they reached the pond at the other end of the park, Eve took out the damp bread and released Tilly from the straps of the pushchair. Standing at the edge of the pond they looked for their favourite duck and Tilly started throwing the bread into the water.

'There he is,' shouted Tilly and Eve looked up to see the green duck making its way over. 'Hello green duck. Here you are.' Tilly threw down some bread near him and squealed with delight as he started to peck it from the ground by her feet.

Later they sat in the warmer side of the covered shelter, out of the wind, to eat their lunch. Tilly enjoyed the soup from her Peppa Pig mug and ate her sandwich, chattering away between mouthfuls. Eve knew she was really blessed. Whatever happened this afternoon didn't matter. She was managing on her own to look after her daughter, however hard it was. She thought back to last year when Ian had still been with them. They had spent a ridiculous amount of money on presents for Tilly and they'd cooked enough food to last them the week. Missing him had become more of a dull ache within her and not the sharp pain it had been in the first few months. She mustn't think of it today. She took out the letter and read it again. Her father had invited them over and suggested two o'clock as the time they should call. She had missed him too. It was her father who had brought her up. He had been a good father lavishing time on her. He had supported her in all the activities she'd wanted to try, discussed her homework with her, showed her the magic of theatre and even helped her learn to play the flute. They had argued about literature, politics and even food. She could see now he had been helping her develop a critical mind. He had been a wonderful dad.

'This afternoon we've got a special treat. We're going to your granddad's house. He has invited us over. You haven't met him before but I'm sure he'll love meeting you.'

'Granddad's house,' Tilly repeated happily. 'Oh look, green duck,' Tilly pointed to the ground. 'Can we take him with us?'

'No, he needs to stay near the pond. He's a naughty boy, isn't he? He keeps coming to join us for our picnics when we come here.' They fed him some more bread and walked him back to the pond before they left the park.

At two o'clock on the dot Eve knocked on her father's front door. It was the first time she'd visited in three years; since she'd run away from home with Ian. Her father had warned her that he'd have nothing to do with her if she carried on seeing Ian and he'd been as good as his word. It had shocked her when he'd shut her out of his life, but each time she had written to him, he had put her letter in an envelope and sent it back to her. And he had been right. Ian had conned people out of money, got himself into fights and then run off with a girl called Tania, who was still at school.

The door opened and Mrs Hood, her father's housekeeper grinned at her.

'Come along in child. So this must be Tilly. What a little poppet she is. Your dad's in the front room.'

Eve helped Tilly out of the pushchair and took a deep breath as she opened the front room door. Her father was standing at the other side of the room. They hesitated for just a moment and then he moved towards her and gave her a hug.

'Good to see you Evie and is this Tilly?'

Tilly darted behind her and clutched her legs.

'She's just a little shy. Give her a few minutes.'

'Would you like to see what's under my Christmas tree, Tilly?' he asked. She peeped round and looked at him and then at the tree.

'Shall we all take a look?' said Eve taking Tilly's hand. Soon they were sitting round the fire opening presents. There was a small parcel for Eve and two larger ones for Tilly.

'Would you like to give your Granddad this present?' Eve said. Shyly Tilly went over and gave him the little package. It was a small picture of Tilly in a recycled frame, but it looked good and meant she had not come empty handed.

'Thank you so much, Tilly,' said Granddad with the biggest smile on his face.

The first present that Tilly opened was a beautiful fairy tree house. Eve took one look at it and found herself crying. All the hardship of the past year came to her; the scrimping and scrapping and how Ian had so completely deserted them. She wiped her face so that her daughter wouldn't see her cry.

'Is something wrong with the present Eve?' her father asked, full of concern.

'Not a thing. I bought her two little fairies for Christmas and I wanted to get her the tree house for them, but well, I couldn't. It's a perfect present.' She took the fairies out of her bag and gave them to Tilly, who became completely engrossed in the magical land of fairies.

After a while Tilly opened the second present and there was a soft cuddly green duck.

'How could you possible know about green duck?' Eve asked.

'About a fortnight ago, I was sitting in the park in the shelter and I heard you and Tilly talking, from the other side. I recognised your voice immediately. Green duck had joined you for lunch and I gather he had most of your sandwich,' said Granddad. 'When your letter arrived, telling me Ian had gone and asking to visit, I persuaded Mrs Hood to make it for me. Seems to be a hit!'

They both looked at Tilly who was cuddling green duck to death.

'Tea's up,' Mrs Hood called round the door. 'Are we all ready?'

'Tea's up and milk for me?' asked Tilly.

'As much as you like,' said Mrs Hood.

'C'mon Granddad. Tea's up,' Tilly said as she took Eve's hand to follow Mrs Hood.

The dining room table was laden with goodies. There were plates of ham and cheese and sausage rolls, cakes of all shapes and sizes and everything was set out beautifully. At the end of the table there was even a high chair. It was a proper Christmas feast. Eve smiled. She may have very little money but Tilly was having a brilliant Christmas.

Later as Mrs Hood was talking to Tilly, her dad had a chance to talk to Eve.

'I'm sorry that Ian left you. You know I thought he was no good, but that's in the past. You're welcome here anytime, and if you wanted to move back in, there's plenty of space. I rattle round in this old place, even with Mrs Hood to keep me company.'

'Thanks Dad. Not sure about moving back home. I like my own space and it might take Tilly a little time to get to know you properly.'

'Peep bo,' shouted Tilly peeking round the side of her mug and looking at her Granddad.

'Peep bo,' shouted Granddad back. Eve smiled at her dad. It looked as if her daughter had decided Granddad was fun. Eve slipped off her shoes under the table and stretched her toes. It felt so good to be home.

Sample story from Pebble on a Beach by Penny Luker.

The Original Species

Elinor balanced the book on her head until she was far enough down the stepladder to land the book on the desk. A small cloud of dust immediately went up in the air and was visible in the light streaming in from the window. Taking a seat at the large oak desk, she opened the book carefully and began hunting for a zebrule. Images of sepia coloured animals and carefully drawn black and white ones, swept before her eyes.

'There it is,' she thought, 'the hybrid of a zebra and a mule, half covered with stripes. It was just like the picture her colleague Mike had sent her. These accidents of nature happened now and again in the wild but it meant the creature was quite rare.

Having identified the animal wouldn't help Mike a lot. A local tribe, in Africa where he was working, wanted to kill the animal for its coat, but Mike with his passion for animals would find a way to protect it. She had no doubt about that.

Elinor continued to browse through the old book. She loved it. Being a zodiographer herself, she enjoyed seeing how her grandfather and his generation had meticulously recorded every new species they could find and how they had made names for themselves in the process. If the photographs were unclear or nobody had been able to take one they had drawn the animals seen on their research trips with amazingly accurate detail. There

127

was little chance of finding new species these days but as she loved the study of animals and nature for its own sake she was not bothered about becoming famous.

She flicked her blonde hair out of her eyes and decided that she would wash and clean up the specimen that Mike had sent her, currently residing in the spare freezer in the cellar. Knowing him he would have bagged and crated it up as soon as it had been killed by the locals, probably having to give them a bribe so that he could keep it. If she cleaned it up now, she could photograph it and check her books tonight to see if she could identify it. Tomorrow she would go into the University's lab. The creature would have sufficiently defrosted to be put through the scanner machine. Then she'd be able to see its insides without cutting it up and it could be preserved for future study.

Donning some clean green scrubs, which she'd inherited from her days working as a vet, she secured a mask over her mouth and set up her mobile phone as a Dictaphone. She slipped on latex gloves and went to lift the crated package from the chest freezer. It was cold in the cellar where she worked. Not quite so cold that you could see your breath, but uncomfortable nevertheless. Prizing off the outer wooden casing, Elinor unwrapped the creature. She poured a bowl of cold water and using a sterile sponge, cleaned the small rodent like body. It was the size of a squirrel and its eyes were unnervingly wide open. She felt almost as if she was being watched. She examined the creature carefully but there was no sign of a wound. Perhaps it had died of natural causes.

The room was uncannily quiet as she photographed the creature with the beautiful gem like eyes. Her new digital camera, although small was of an excellent quality. The camera reflected in the creature's eyes making them appear like emeralds. Having photographed every angle, she was quite sure that she had not seen this animal before. She went to leave the cellar, but on glancing back saw its forlorn little body lying starkly on the bench, so she wrapped it in a wodge of cotton wool and placed it carefully in half of the wooden crate. In her usual untidy manner she left the bowl of water on the bench and the gloves discarded by its side.

From the starkness of the cellar room she was pleased to return to her large comfortable, warm study. Three walls were lined with bookshelves, floor to ceiling. The fourth wall contained the fire, which was lit in the grate and was the focal point of the room. Nearby was a dark green leather sofa. Elinor ignored that. She heaved the antique book from her desk so that it was by the fire. Then she picked up a crimson embroidered cushion, and stuffed it between her back and the sofa and started to hunt for the creature through the yellowed pages. The book provided no answers, which meant that Elinor had to hit the internet to continue her search. She worked late into the night, but with no luck.

Living alone in her small house had never bothered Elinor. She was quite happy with her own company and a good book, but as she went upstairs to bed she suddenly felt for the first time that she was not entirely alone.

In the morning she cradled her coffee cup in her hands to warm them as she went downstairs to the cellar. She picked up the other half of the crate and placed it carefully over the creature. Then she went to throw away the water in the bowl but there was none. Elinor shrugged and picked up the gloves to bin them but they fell apart in her hand. 'Mice,' she thought and left the room with the little box.

The lab was bright and white and immaculate. It was a privilege to have access to such facilities. She had booked an hour in the scanner suite, to examine her specimen and as it remained unidentified she hoped the inner picture would provide some sort of clue as to what it was.

'Well that's odd,' she thought as she opened the box. 'It's lying on its front but I placed it on its back. Oh I'm completely mad; I must have opened the box upside down.'

She took out the little body and placed it on the scanner. Then she went into the next room to watch the images come through. It was nothing like the insides of anything she had seen before. The images started at the feet but when they reached what should have been the digestive area there were two heart like organs. These images were not clear.

'Oh are you scanning a live animal?' Nadine, the laboratory assistant, asked her.

Elinor was about to say no, when she realized that maybe she was. As soon as the machine switched off she went in and picked up the inert body to feel if it was warm, but it was cold. She looked again into the reflective eyes.

'You are going to kill me, aren't you?' a voice said inside her head. It was a shock to realize the creature was communicating with her. She found her hands were sweating and wiped them down her jeans.

'No, but where are you from?' she asked.

'I live a far distance from your Earth. I come from one of the moons of the planet you call Jupiter. You will want to cut me up to see how I work. I have seen it in your science books.'

'Jupiter? I didn't think life was possible there. Oh my goodness I have so many questions. I can't believe you are alive. Oh this is so exciting. I do want to know how you survive and oh I have loads to ask. Listen I'm going to put you back in the crate and take you back to my home. There are some here who might want to have a good look at you, so it'll be safer there. Once we get home we'll decide how to help you.'

Quickly Elinor downloaded the scanned images onto a pen drive and deleted them from the university's computer. She carried the crate under one arm and passed Nadine on the way out.

'Did you find out what it was?' Nadine asked.

'Yes, it was a common African rodent. I'm just going to take it home and write it up for Mike as part of his visit. See you next week.'

On arriving home, Elinor went into her library and undid the crate. She lifted out the creature.

'What can I do to make you comfortable and well?' she asked.

'I will recover slowly as I wake up properly. We sleep for many of your years at a time and as we sleep our body temperature falls below zero,' she heard. 'I have had so little sleep.'

'Would you like some water?'

'Yes and thank you. And I want to know why you are not going to kill me and become famous, like your grandfather for discovering new species?'

'You're a living creature, just like me and I write about animals because they fascinate me. You could tell me all about yourself and where you live and I promise I will never publish the information until we've got you safely home.'

'If you publish then my home won't be safe.'

'What if you tell me your story and I write it as a story, not as a fact? Nobody will ever guess that I've really met an alien and I can always change the planet you really come from.'

And the little creature, with deep soulful eyes, looked into Elinor's crystal blue ones and saw the same love of life that he had. Both scientists in their different ways, they told their stories to worlds that listened fascinated, but never for one moment suspected the truth.

***

More books by this author

Pebble on a Beach
Short stories for adults

Nature's Gold, Autumn Gold and The Shadow of Love, are collections of poetry.

The Truth Finder is a Young Adult Fantasy

Children's Books
The Green Book
Tiny Tyrannosaurus
Desdemona: The dragon without any friends

www.pennyluker.wordpress.com

Made in the USA
Las Vegas, NV
22 March 2022

46108654R00075